# Nephilim Awakened

# Nephilim Awakened

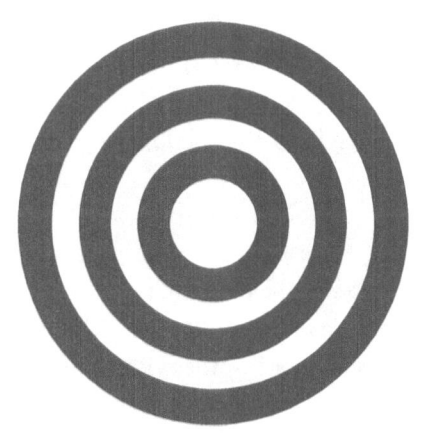

## Joanne Johnson

Published by Falkor Publishing, an Auryn Creative imprint.
www.falkorpublishing.com

Edited by Tanis Glenn
Cover illustration by Maureen Shockey
Book design by Carlos Moreno

ISBN 978-0-615-61557-8

www.nephilimawakened.com

## ACKNOWLEDGEMENTS

I thank Jim Goodgion, Lissa Mallory, Rebecca McGinty, David Braun, Don Moye', Adrienne Reneau, Joan Houser, and Kevin Scarboro for their helpful critiques.

I especially thank my husband Rod for his continued support, love, and patience throughout this endeavor.

# 1. HANK, THE FARMER

I MET HIM ONE DAY on my daily walk. It was the same route I always took past the pecan grove and the large horse ranch, ending at the base of a majestic, snow-capped mountain. It wasn't that I actually enjoyed this diligent hour of self-torture. But it did bring a kind of satisfaction being disciplined in this one thing in my life.

It was a pleasant, sunny day in late October when our worlds collided. There he stood next to his bicycle with a flat. He was an elderly, thin man of six feet or more with dirty overalls and a badly frayed straw hat shading an unshaven face. He looked homeless.

"Need some air in that tire?" I offered.

"No, think I'll just walk it on home from here. But thank you, Miss."

"But my house is right there," I said, pointing to the left.

We walked to my little adobe retreat which was hidden from the world behind towering agave. He used my air pump. We exchanged first names, then sat in brightly painted rocking chairs and enjoyed a glass of cold iced tea with fresh mint from my garden. He didn't seem in a hurry to get home and frankly I enjoyed the company. Hank was educated and cautious. I quickly raised him from the level of homeless to eccentric and pictured him living in a vintage travel trailer hidden away on a ranch where he had menial chores allowing him to live the rest of his life peacefully, alone.

Our conversation took several friendly, but shallow routes until eventually I asked him about his past occupations, wondering if he had any. He claimed he had farmed nine hundred acres along the outskirts of the White Sands Missile Range for thirty years. He paused a moment carefully planning what to say next.

"I had crops and cattle, but my Herefords kept roaming into the restricted area. I sold out and moved here," he explained.

I quickly imagined possible ways he could have squandered his money leaving him in this state and concluded he had an addiction.

He darted his eyes at me. 'It's a lie,' I thought.

I had nothing to lose now so I questioned if he ever saw anything strange out there, hoping he would entertain me with exciting, mysterious tales.

"Sometimes," he responded quietly.

Perhaps I had hit a chord, because he then stood up and politely thanked me for the air. I watched as he cycled off down the same road we had met on.

'Well, you sure blew that,' I thought to myself. A nagging feeling of unfinished business or something I needed to remember tortured me into the night.

The next morning, I grabbed my straw hat and walked to the library with the intention of finding a good book to help pass idle hours. The building's quaint appearance with bright blue doors and an orange bench placed thoughtfully under a pecan tree welcomed me. I especially enjoyed the whimsical life-size ceramic donkey painted in a multitude of cheerful colors that stood proudly in its courtyard. This was one of the appreciated, enhanced aspects of our little New Mexico village.

While combing the shelves, dusty like the rest of the town, I was distracted by glass shattering outside. The librarian was an obese female Native American who completely swallowed up her desk chair while seated. Her glossy, black hair was knotted neatly at the back of her head. I often admired the long, colorful print skirts she always wore. She had slanting dark eyes that swept the perimeter of the library from time to time over tiny spectacles. At the sound of this breaking glass, she jumped up, waddled to the front door at an alarming speed, and flung it open.

"Get out of here you dried up old prune-faced piece of white trash or I'll scalp you slowly with a dull knife!" she yelled.

I immediately forgot my quest for a book. I waited until I heard her chair moan and squeak from her settling and bravely stepped out from between the bookshelves. With a 'save my ass smile,' I made a quick exit through the front door. I wasn't disappointed in how this day was turning out.

Work ethic was not a requirment in this insignificant, desert town. Indians reigned here and I was a minority. So was Hank.

Like an exciting novel warming up, I saw Hank pedaling away as fast as his old bony legs could manage. My curiosity was piqued and I decided to follow. Being in fairly good shape, I kept pace. I turned down a lane that led to the horse ranch at the end of my road. There, nestled in on the side of a large, well-maintained barn and under a shady tree, was an old Airstream trailer with his bicycle leaning against it. Not such a bad deal, I thought. A rusty metal chair and table were placed nearby, where he probably sat on lazy afternoons eating stolen pecans.

I wasn't through looking. I stepped behind a large tree trunk on the opposite side of the lane, not wanting him to catch me in my childish snooping. What first appeared to be junk in his modest, borrowed front yard began to take on new meaning as I stared at the pieces of tires, bottles, tin cans, etc. Was it recycled art? There were three distinct formations possessing a vague familiarity. I had seen enough. I knew where he lived.

Later, while performing my nightly ritual of nodding off to the 10 o'clock news, I was startled by the sound of a flowerpot crashing on the front porch followed by shuffling footsteps. I quickly grabbed my cell phone dialed 911 with one hand while retrieving my small pistol from a drawer under the lamp. I had been told there was no need to lock your doors here, but now I was glad my big city ways hadn't abandoned me yet. Hearing the dipatcher at the police station on the line gave me the courage to peek through the blinds. Revolving, bright lights blinded me and flooded the yard. I reminded myself the police department, and everything else in this town was only one block away. I watched as someone darted a flashlight here and there, then came a loud knock at the door.

A stocky Apache disguised as a policeman asked me the usual mundane questions. His impersonal, disinterested manner annoyed me so I asked him if this sort of thing happened often. He never looked up, but said, "Sometimes."

I locked both doors, closed and locked all the windows, got comfortable on the couch where I could maintain a central visual, and tried to get some rest, with the lamp on and the pistol still in my hand. I drifted off in short increments, not able to sleep more than one to two hours at a time.

I was thankful for morning and took my coffee to the usual place, the porch swing. The crisp, fall air was filled with the fresh scent of sage. With a warm throw over my shoulders, I suspiciously scoped my front yard. Everything seemed normal. The three foot adobe wall defining the edge of my porch was still adorned with potted geraniums and aloe vera. The stone pathway leading to the old, iron gate seemed intact. My blooming white-tufted evening primrose and hybrid tea roses appeared undisturbed on either side of the path.

I didn't see any footsteps in the sandy soil. Whoever had come here had walked carefully on the stones. I glanced over at the broken clay pot that left dirt and aloe vera scattered everywhere. I had meant to move that plant, but now placed another in exactly the same inconvenient place. As I swept the porch, a vision from a dream the night before danced across my mind. I held on to it before it disappeared. It had been about one of Hank's sculptures. Of course, that was it! The art was the same shape as the tall, shadowed visitors in my recurring nightmare. It was my personal hell, this disgusting dream of mine, following me everywhere. It always ended with me waking up in a loud scream. I quickly dismissed it from my mind. But there was something else. Had I really seen a faint blue aura linger near my gate before the policeman entered the yard? It had happened so quickly.

The next day, anxious to resume life as normal, I walked to the farmers market. Defiantly, I let the screen door slam behind me announcing my new found freedom to the world. My inheritance had allowed me the time to enjoy life as I pleased. I recently had chosen to take off a year before deciding what to do. Six months had passed and I still had no thoughts on the subject. Moving to this quaint village I had visited on several previous vacations offered me a different rhythm of life that I had remembered and cherished from my childhood. The slow pace, I admit, had been challenging as I adjusted.

This was the day local farmers spread their brightly colored vegetables and fruit on tables in the park. I browsed, happily squeezing the fruit for the ripest selections, when I heard someone behind me say, "Why did you follow me yesterday?"

I dropped the oranges I was holding and watched them roll away in all directions. I thought for a second before turning around. I was caught. Even my 'save my ass smile' was of no use now. I turned slowly and looked up into Hank's eyes, searching.

"Because I was bored and wanted to see where you lived?"

'I should have lied,' I thought. The truth didn't sound convincing enough.

"Why didn't you just ask me when I was with you the other day?" he replied, annoyed.

"You left so fast I forgot to ask you. I was curious and there's not much to do here." I answered.

He wasn't buying any of it and my face was now beet red.

"Who do you work for?" he asked, still agitated with me.

"I don't work," I said. "Who do you think I work for?"

I was growing tired of this game so I stood up taller and asked him if he had come into my yard the night before around ten thirty and if so, did he see a strange aura of blue lingering near my gate. I could tell that I had hit another chord, but I plowed through. "Why do you have supernatural and other worldly symbols in your yard as recycled art forms?"

With that, his eyes widened and he almost stumbled backwards. An uncomfortable pause followed. "Quickly, come with me," he said, taking my arm.

I reluctantly let him lead me to a park bench away from the market. Hank was old and frail, I assured myself. Besides, another Apache warrior disguised as a policeman was taking his lunch nearby. He was eating the typical local favorite: fry bread with chili on top. It smelled wonderful.

Not sure of Hank's sanity, I studied him as his demeanor changed drastically. He got my full attention when he pulled out an intricate small device I hadn't even known was on the market yet. As he looked down at it I wondered if he was using it to scan his e-mails or me. He shoved it back in his pocket and quickly surveyed the park.

'This village is anything but boring,' I thought.

"Okay, here's the deal," he said, sitting down next to me. "If you recognize the symbols in my yard, then you know things."

"Know what things?" I asked him.

"Lets start over," he said. "Tell me what the symbols mean to you."

I began describing the one that reminded me of the symbol for Alpha and Omega, the embodiment of All. "The one that borhers me is the shape you achieved suggesting tall, thin dark humanoids. I admit your use of wine bottles and plastic crates is clever, but it reminds me of a frightening, recurring nightmare I've been having." He looked at me with renewed interest as I rambled on. "The last one was easy. I saw particles and waves basically representative of what all things are made of. How did I do?" I finished.

He didn't reply, but instead asked me if I had ever experienced a floating sensation when I slept. I nodded slowly wondering how he was aware of this very private part of my life.

"I hate it. I'm hanging in the air near the ceiling facing my bed. I angrily demand they put me down. Then I wake up in my bed. I have no idea who they are, and I've never told anyone."

"Look," he said, "there's a simple explanation for all that. It's not as bad as you think."

"How do you know?" I demanded.

"Because I'm a Quantum Mechanics Specialist and my position

is one of diplomacy among several species," he said, handing me his business card.

With that being said, I bolted up and began running home. He followed me on his bicycle like a never-ending bad dream.

"You need to come to my R.V. for your vaccines!" he yelled.

"Nope, but thanks for the invite," I hollered back as I ran up to my door. I didn't want Hank for an enemy, and was unsure if his diagnosis made him dangerous or not. Relieved to be inside, I locked the door behind me. What had begun as entertaining was now turning ugly. I had had enough and felt threatened.

I heard a repeated soft knocking at the door. I started to dial 911 and I'm still not sure what stopped me. Instead, I stood before the door and listened.

"You were just returning from a quantum leap, only something disturbed you normal pattern. It frightens you to find yourself in that state, floating like that.

"The figures in my yard are Ziots from the planet Zio, which is in a parallel universe. They are peaceful, advanced extraterrestrial beings that probably assist you in returning home. You see them observing you there - not here. They know where you came from, can easily find you, but aren't the least bit interested in following you to your home planet. We can talk more about this experience if you want, but I strongly suggest you receive necessary inoculations if you are transiting between planets alone. I would like to talk to you more at another time. You might be an unsuspecting descendant of very special origins."

"Go away Hank," I said.


The next day I hammered a sign into the ground with great deliberation. It read: *FOR SALE BY OWNER.*

# 2. ZIO

I THREW MYSELF INTO MINDLESS HOUSEWORK hoping it would help me forget the past two days. It was working until I heard tapping on my living room window. I had no time to hide and was pretty sure he spotted me dusting furniture. I walked to the window and looked him square in the eyes. "What now, Hank? Will you please just leave me alone?"

He had a look about him like a mad scientist, with a wild look in his eyes and terrible bed hair. He began to ramble, talking loudly through the window. "Here on earth, scientists are just beginning to understand the Quantum Leap Theory and the nature of particles and waves that make up matter. Physicists are in the process of revising their basic concepts of space, time, gravitation, and the nature of the cosmos as a whole. They are only at the tip of the iceberg though. The psyche, you see, is involved with the determination of the observed properties."

"Are you even aware you are trespassing and harassing me?" I threatened. "Get to the point. I have things to do."

"What I came here to tell you is that your visitor the other night was most likely a Dhakart. They are a harmless, clumsy lot - very advanced, but terribly nosey. They spend a lot of time keeping track of other planets and their progress. They haven't mastered adapting to this environment completely and leave a blue aura behind." Hank chuckled to himself.

"However, the main reason I insist on bothering you is that I believe you are in grave danger and the Dhakart's presence only assures me of this. I have found out that since yesterday your whereabouts are being tracked."

The persistent feeling that I needed to remember something returned. It was how my intuition worked. I knew something, but I didn't consciously know what it was. It was a terrible nagging feeling that alluded to trouble coming my way. I threw the feather duster on the coffee table and sat down on the couch under the window, giving in to his rambling.

"Are you aware of the importance of your ability to travel through space and time, and that there are certain secret factions of our own government that track people like yourself for valuable, scientific research?" I knew he was right. I decided to let him come inside.

I opened the door slowly with my pistol in my hand. He stepped back with an alarmed look on his face. I silently pointed my pistol to the rocking chair near the fireplace. He nodded, and humbly scurried across the living room to the chair.

"Let's back up a bit," I interjected. "You said you worked with other species?"

"Yes, that's correct," he confirmed. "There are underground

tunnels and stations beneath the missile range as well as many other locations all over the world. At this particular site, I assisted scientists in understanding particles and waves. They were about to understand grasp how moving through space and time utilizing special gateways worked when the Dhakarts stopped us and moved the entire station through kinetics. It was gone in seconds. They made a deal with us. They stated that earthlings lacked the necessary advancement spiritually and intellectually to be trustworthy enough to gain access to other inhabited planets. There was nothing we could do, so we promised to discontinue our research. They, in turn, gave us knowledge to harness power from water and our own magnetic field, because we were damaging our environment to the point of no return on our present course. They want to continue using our large supply of water from oceans, lakes, and rivers to fuel their spacecraft."

"What does all this have to do with me?" I asked.

"Well, the Dhakarts were right. You see, our government has continued this research, albeit in a different, more destructive way. When they find someone like yourself who can quantum leap, they turn them into a lab rat. I've seen how they destroy for their own purpose with little regard for life. I was present when they tore apart a Dhakart in Roswell. They didn't even bother giving him anesthesia before cutting him open."

I asked Hank in a trembling voice, "What should I do?"

"Go to the planet Zio, where you've been before. There's a reason you go there, by the way. Fall asleep and trust your instincts. The Ziots will understand what's in your heart and you can remain there. There are already many others like you living there and you will adjust effortlessly. Living among Ziots comes with perks. They will individualize a perfect diet for you and your health will be flawlessly maintained. After your orientation, if there is time, you will be encouraged to study a subject of your own interest as long as you use it to serve the universe in a positive way."

Suddenly there was the sound of a rotorcraft approaching. Hank jumped up. I did the same, dropping my pistol on the floor. I quickly put it back in the drawer and joined him at the window. The rotorcraft was almost overhead now.

Excitedly, Hank pointed to the far corner of the living room and said, "Stand over there where there's nothing of interest for them to search. I'm going to put you in an invisible field. You can't move or it will dissolve and you'll be caught. It will be very cold, but you must not move if you want to live."

I did want to live and tried desperately not to tremble. Tiny, prickly vibrations began traveling my skin from head to toe. I was just getting used to it when the front door flew open with a loud THUG! I took very slow, shallow breaths and stared at a picture on the opposite wall and tried not to blink. There were five figures in black uniforms. I read the letters NSB on a helmet as one passed me. He stopped, picking up my voice-controlled wristband cellphone off of the coffee table and checked the last time I had received a call. Luckily, nobody had called since yesterday. He took it. Another found my pistol, and took that also. Just as he turned, I saw the words *New Science Bureau* above his pocket. They searched the house, spending the most time in my bedroom looking through my chest of drawers, pictures, and probably searching pockets in the closet. I couldn't imagine any other reason to take so long going through my clothes. Someone grabbed my mail off of the desk and stuffed it in his pocket.

I was growing numb from the piercing cold and trying

desperately not to tremble when one of them motioned to the others to leave. I let my teeth chatter as I listened to the rotorcraft drift away. I quickly grabbed a throw from nearby, wrapped it around me, and ran to the bathroom for a hot shower.

Later that evening, I let my body sink into my not so new, but comfortable couch. Exhausted, I wept. I didn't spend time trying to figure out how Hank had managed to disappear without using the front door. Nor did I care to dwell on something Hank had said. The phrase, 'if there's time' bothered me. What had he meant?

Guess I can't take a suitcase with me. How do I notify family and friends? If I left a note, what would it say? "Gone to Zio, back soon!" How did I get myself into this terrible situation? I finally gave up torturing myself and got comfortable listening to the quiet. My inner voice said, 'Just let go.' I fell asleep.

Surprisingly, I found myself in a pleasant, lucid dream. The night sky was alive with purple, blue, and soft hues of pink floating in and out of the darkness like the aurora borealis. The moon reflected a constantly changing kaleidoscope of colors. I stood on a beach of pure white sand watching all the colors from the sky reflected in slow, lazy waves gently ending at my feet. There was movement down the beach in the distance. Something tall and thin was moving ... no, gliding ... towards me. I ran from it towards the dunes, climbing each one and sometimes falling down the other side until I was far beyond it. I now felt cool, green grass beneath my bare feet. Someone behind me said, "Welcome." I turned quickly and there before my eyes was the very outline of the dark shadowy form, just like the visitors from the dreams I've had since childhood;

a tall, thin humanoid with huge eyes. Paralyzed with fear, I watched as he reached down and gently took my hand with his long, thin fingers. I tried to protest, but instead an unexpected calmness swept over me. "Welcome to Zio," he said, without using words.

"Do you see the soft lights from the transparent dome higher up in those mountains?" he asked. I was rudely staring at him with my mouth still open. He politely and calmly allowed me the time to adjust to the sight of him. His skin had a translucent quality that made me think his true nature might be invisible. His head was large in proportion to his body. His eyes were huge dark sockets of total blackness, and yet I felt a sense of compassion and love emanating from them. "Let us go there now," he said, in his telepathic way of communicating. He took my hand and we seemed to transport instantly to the inside of an elaborate crystal building.

"All the beauty and benefits your world offers have been re-created here for you and the others." I wondered where the others were. The landscaping inside was lush to say the least. Small streams winding under walkways trickled over smooth stones. The air smelled clean. Dark green foliage lined the halls.

I was already getting used to his gliding just above the ground, but could be difficult to keep up. Next, we came to a massive indoor garden. I understood him to convey that I would never eat meat again. Suddenly, I felt a craving for a thick grilled steak and lobster. He smiled. He had read my thoughts. Thank goodness, I thought, there's humor here.

A startling, piercing, shriek made my heart leap. I covered my ears and looked up, seeing an eagle soaring over the dome. The Ziot explained that many endangered species from my planet had been brought here and lived in a protected habitat farther away.

As we walked beyond the garden I wondered why I still hadn't seen 'the others.' We passed through a motion-sensor door, in to what appeared to be living quarters. An orange mist bathed me as I entered. I couldn't help noticing how much better I felt. He explained that it was a cell renewal mist. Maybe it was, but my guess was that it was a disinfectant to ward off earthly germs and maybe a little 'feel good' something for me, too. I realized that this would be my personal space. I wasn't comfortable with such easy access to my room from the outside. He explained that it was a DNA-sensitive entry and was transparent only from the inside, allowing me to view anyone asking permission to enter.

"A soft chime will be heard if someone approaches," he continued. "To open the door for a visitor you need only nod. It will open immediately for you as you near it."

I stepped back, analyzing him again. I felt sure Ziots were ethereal, and his form was a kind of polite gesture giving me something tangible to visualize. Everything caught up to me at once. I felt lightheaded. I walked up to a platform suspended in air about 3 feet high. It had caught my attention when we first entered the room. It seemed to be made of a clear substance resembling glass and slowly changed colors. The being suggested I lie down on it. When I did, it gently conformed to my body. It was the most comfortable bed I had ever experienced. I wondered what kept it in the air like that.

After a few moments, I rose to take in the rest of my surroundings. A huge black wall took up half of the living area. Placed in front of this wall was a plush, white reclining chair with buttons on one of the arms. I was prompted to try it out and when I reclined in it, a small keyboard rose from one side.

The Ziot merely pointed to several buttons and suddenly my old adobe home in New Mexico appeared larger than life, there on the black wall. I saw NSB government agents swarming my house again. What were they searching for? 'I should have left that note,' I thought.

So this was my media screen and where I would learn. I saw Hank sitting under his tree eating pecans. I was pretty sure he stole them from the grove nearby on a regular basis. He made a symbol with his fingers and the Ziot returned it. I realized now his importance as an ambassador of peace. He had chosen to live the way he did, placing no value on wealth or conveniences. He then turned and looked right at me smiling. Startled, I lunged out of the chair and the screen immediately went blank. I would need an orientation on how to use it and its capabilities.

The Ziot was so quiet I almost forgot he was there. I heard him say, "In time; slow down."

Exhausted, I felt the urge to move back to my floating 'perfect Serta' which my new friend referred to as my 'resting place.' A feeling of peace came over me as I lay there listening to a soft waterfall and watching representations of seascapes and clouds move gently across the ceiling. The Ziot had disappeared now ... maybe. My eyelids became very heavy and I fell into a much needed deep sleep.

# 3. UNIVERSE GEOGRAPHY

THE NEXT MORNING, I sat up in bed eager to start the first day in this new world. I had slept comfortably in some sort of invisible energy field, that felt like a warm cocoon and replaced the need for my traditional bedding.

After dangling my legs over the side of my suspended bed for a minute, yawning and stretching, I hopped to the floor. Through squinting eyes, I noticed a private garden for the first time through an opaque wall. Beyond this was a white wall about eight feet tall. I wondered what the wall was keeping out.

Curious to explore more of my space, I approached a door in an archway on the other side of the room that silently slid open for me. Just beyond it, I found an uncluttered closet with simple, yet attractive, garments and three pairs of shoes. I quickly changed into a plain, turquoise, loose fitting garment with a metallic sheen.

A pair of soft shoes with generously padded sole were probably for walking and daily wear. Another pair had a more rugged appearance with a bright yellow, thick-treaded sole at least 5 inches tall. There were no shoelaces. Curious, I slid my feet into them and they slowly started conforming to my feet. When they stopped moving, I jumped up in them to try them out.

That was a mistake. I hit my head on the ceiling and soon learned that I had begun an uncontrollable process. My shoes immediately returned my body to the floor. I was in a daze, but the bouncing was not over. Next, they sent me flying through a second archway where I landed in a swimming pool—soaking wet, confused and feeling foolish. I slowly came to the understanding that this room I had flown into was a well-equipped spa complete with a massage table, a plush white lounge chair, and a tropical greenhouse.

Suddenly, someone entered the bathroom through the wall and began walking toward me. Her appearance was somewhat comical. She looked to be about 25 years old, maybe 5'7" tall, had florescent, short green hair, and was clothed in a snug, silky jumpsuit of bright magenta. I laughed—then stopped abruptly, remembering my manners. I felt like I was in an old 70s sci-fi movie.

"Hello. My name is Amie," she introduced.

I ditched the shoes and tried to escape towards the closet area. She reappeared on the other side of me. My heart was pounding as I attempted normal conversation fully aware now that I could not outrun her. "Amie, where is the bathroom?" I asked tentatively.

"There," she replied, pointing back to the room with the pool.

"Is this pool the bathtub then?"

"Certainly," she replied, "and it is also your Jacuzzi." I noted a slight accent when she spoke. I decided to keep her engaged in conversation while I planned my escape, thinking she surely had to be a little off, dressed like that and all.

"Amie, where is the toilet?"

She walked over to a small square located on the floor and as she approached, a crescent moon about 2½ feet long and 1½ foot wide rose before her. "You sit here," she said. "After you stand up, it will drop beneath the floor and self-clean."

"Okay." Something was strange about her. I thanked her for her assistance and said I did not want to take up anymore of her time. She got the point and quickly disappeared back into the wall.

What a relief, I thought. She's gone! Who is she? I wasn't comfortable with her easy access to my room. I ran back to the living area to call for help, but when I opened my mouth nothing came out. A slip of paper on my bed caught my attention.

Who had entered my room? Was it her? Did she have access to me through any wall? I examined the paper, which looked like an itinerary of daily activities. So this was no simple vacation after all. The page consisted of some symbols I didn't recognize and a daily schedule divided into breakfast, research/education, meditation, spiritual enlightenment, lunch, physical fitness, and so on. What would happen if I just took the day off? I noticed there were certain days marked for tours of Zio with a reminder to wear my 'leaping shoes.' I was very sure which ones those were. I wondered where I would be leaping.

Further down the page was the name, AMIE. I read the following:

*Amie is your personal assistant. She is an A-7856 Android pxl. She has the ability to answer questions on any subject, translate symbols and languages, explain equations and scientific problems, and adapt to your learning style. She will tidy up your personal space, and prepare your meals. She is a trained herbalist, with a complete knowledge of homeopathic cures for all human ailments, and she can give healing massages. All physical data relating to your health is recorded through eye contact with her daily. She is programmed to protect you and is equipped with a gun, and missiles, although she is lethal with or without weapons. Amie is void of emotion and therefore is not interested in being your friend. Ironically however, she IS your best friend must always travel with you outside the perimeters of your area. Don't leave home without her.*

I now had a higher regard for Amie, but thought it best to wait on a massage.

A loud roar overhead quickly averted my attention. Just above the other dome were strange looking vessels emitting red and blue streams of color. I saw repeated white sparks and ribbons of green light in the sky.

Something black and ugly was crawling over the white wall and in to my space! My heart beating wildly I dove under the bed, realizing too late that I was completely visible there. I wanted to move, but felt too paralyzed with fear.

A creature resembling a huge bat was using its wings to pull himself along, searching the garden. It spotted me! I screamed and Amie was suddenly in front of me. She shot her laser gun through the opaque wall at the creature and instructed me not to look at it no matter what happened. I heard more 'zing' noises from the gun. The wall mended itself after each shot, making a squishy, slippery sound. The creature retreated back up the white wall … and I looked. It was bleeding a thick blue substance that dripped into puddles. As it reached the top it turned to look at me with its red eyes. I buried my face in my hands and heard it fall over the wall.

Amie said, "They will steal your power and knowledge leaving you worthless."

"Worthless?" I asked. Maybe she meant brainless. If that bat-thing was looking for my brain, he might be disappointed. I saw the wounded creature fly off with its legs and wings outstretched. Its wing span must have been at least six yards. The sky was quiet now.

"We have many outposts on Zio manned by armies of androids to take care of these unwelcome entities from other galaxies," she continued, in her funny staccato and monotone voice. "They come to steal what we have. You and the others are safe here."

I had to sit down and the floor was the closest thing. My head was reeling and the room was spinning. I heard myself say, "I don't feel good" and blacked out.


Gradually, consciousness returned and hovering over my body, I saw two huge black eye sockets and a large round cranium that narrowed sharply towards the chin. The urge to scream was stifled as I became aware of my new surroundings. The being appeared to be reading a disc about seven inches in diameter that busily traveled in the air above me from head to toe, making a ticking sound. When the disc stopped moving, the being took it and placed it under his arm. He was now standing next to me. I watched him leave.

Amie walked up to me and said, "Today's excitement and your inability to process your first encounter with unwelcome aliens made you temporarily shut down all sensory and mental processing. In other words, you fainted. You have to be checked for a CGI chip."

"What's that?" I asked her.

"It's a microscopic device the bat-like creatures from Vorta-S3 implant through eye contact that transmits your knowledge to them and identifies for future abduction any special abilities you possess."

"Where's the floating doctor and his toy?" I asked her.

In her mechanical voice, Amie responded, "If you are making reference to the highly capable and educated medical expert who was just here, he has returned to his work. On Zio, life is work and work is life."

"I didn't mean to be disrespectful," I said. "I always use humor when I'm overwhelmed."

"Nor I … I will make note of that," she replied, and exited through the wall.

'Hmm, my first bitchy robot,' I thought.

I reflected on the strangeness I was becoming accustomed to in my space-trotting escapades. An empty, growling sensation in my stomach interrupted my thoughts.

Prompted by an overwhelming attack of hunger, I bravely stepped out alone into an unknown, long corridor. Excited over meeting others, I decided to follow the smell of food and take a right. I had walked for quite a while until I heard a sound behind me and turned to see a tall, thin person, possibly

Norwegian or Danish, taking giant steps in my direction. That was one use for the leaping shoes, I noted.

He waved and yelled, "Hurry up or you'll miss breakfast." I started running.

A wonderful aroma indicated I was getting close. I approached a dining room filled with people of all ages. When I entered, they all stood up and began clapping. This helped me feel better. I guessed getting here was quite an accomplishment. Everyone stopped clapping and sat back down, resuming their meal and conversations. Well, after all, they had gotten here the same way.

Breakfast consisted of cereal resembling a robust granola with chunks of fruit and nuts, accompanied by a crude, homemade slice of multi-grain toast with tiny seeds in it. A tall glass of something green was my drink. Everyone looked like normal people from Earth, of all ages and races. I devoured the cereal and bread and took a sip of my green drink. It was not bad. I wondered what was in it.

A lady with short blonde hair leaned over and said, "Don't worry, you'll get used to it. It's made of stuff that will give you energy and increased alertness. You'll like it. It's their 'Zio Special.'"

"How long have you been here?" I asked.

"Oh, about ninety years." She didn't look a day past 30.

I sipped the rest of the green drink.

"Do you like it here?"

She responded with a nod while eating her bread. She looked up and said, "I feel fulfilled and have a purpose in life. You see, I've found the cure for cancer."

"That's incredible! Will you go back to Earth with this discovery?"

"No, not me. I've chosen someone in the field there who will think she discovered it. A Ziot will enlighten her very soon."

A soft chime rang and everyone got up and left. I sat there wondering what to do, but right on cue, Amie entered. "I will show you where to go," she said. I was becoming a little annoyed by this all-knowing, unfeeling, perfect android, although I had no choice but to follow her. As we walked, I noticed I was beginning to feel different. My pace had sped up and my vision was blurry. I took off my glasses and found I could see perfectly without them. I hadn't felt this good since high school. I certainly could get used their 'Zio Special' and the orange renewal mist.

She (or 'it') led me to a room with nothing but an egg-shaped chair in the center. I noticed three symbols and the word *Urantia* over the door as we entered. With a wave of her hand, Amie politely invited me to sit in the egg chair. I was reluctant to do so, wondering if the egg might close and devour me.

A Ziot entered the Urantia Room from above, descending slowly. I sat down in the chair with my mouth open, watching this beautiful creature float down with his arms crossed over his chest and his eyes glowing a fluorescent yellow. I imagined the glowing eyes had something to do with his concentration in performing the descent.

Once the descent was complete he approached me, his eyes darkening. "Welcome." he said.

I assumed he was a different Ziot than my initial encounter (they all looked the same to me) so I just replied, "Thank you." Before, the Ziot would respond to my thoughts instead of my spoken words. It was happening again so I decided to stop keeping track of it. I was getting used to it.

The Ziot presented a hologram to me and suggested I step into it. When I did, it added another dimension, making me feel as if I was present in my own past. I was shown multiple trips I had made to Zio while asleep. Androids would spot me on the radar systems lying on the ground just outside a station and quickly bring me inside their safe zone. I was half awake and half asleep in the mysterious REM sleep stages five and six. I had traveled to Zio in these stages and remained somewhat stuck there until the awakening stage followed. During these visits there had been several Ziots bending over to look at me, then they would send me back to Earth where I would sit up in bed screaming, only to remember the dark shapes of the figures I had seen. I was a frequent visitor to their planet in this manner. I dreaded the experience, not knowing who these strange beings were who kept appearing to me. Even now, I found myself afraid to sleep in the dark.

Next, I saw myself in grade school, removing myself from my present environment mentally and doodling the symbol I had been fond of back then. This repetitive habit I engaged in annoyed my teachers, but they chose to disregard it due to my good grades. I never realized that the true meaning of this symbol was buried deep in my subconscious. I saw the symbol in the hologram and experienced its depth as I looked through the circles to the center one. The Ziot described this symbol as three concentric circles representing the material emblem of the *Trinity* government of all creation.

Next I was shown my last home on Earth. There were several items throughout the home I had either made myself or bought, that now drew my attention. The spiral symbol was displayed in some pieces of sculpture, as well as in one large painting. The symbol also appeared in the three tiles I had chosen that were proudly displayed over the fireplace. I had not been fully aware of my attachment to this symbol until now.

"Your nightly travels through the universe, surrounding yourself with the material emblem of the Trinity government, and quantum leaping during REM sleep are all connected. You will understand this in time," he said.

He then ascended, lightening quick, with his arms crossed over his chest. The hologram had returned to the screen on the wall. I couldn't help but ponder on the strange method of ending conversations on Zio. Was it simply that they were so intelligent that the completion of their purpose for being present was in itself enough and justified their abrupt exits? I remembered a professor I had like that in college. After uttering the very last word of his lesson for that day, he would rudely slam his book closed loudly and exit the room. He was finished, and you were suddenly jolted out of your seat if you had fallen asleep. I was unusually attentive in this class, trying to guess his completion before he slammed the book closed.

Amie returned, and I asked her why the Ziot had left. She explained that he decided that no more information was necessary now because it would overwhelm me. I followed her out the door and down the hall, then she invited me to enter a different room, using the same little polite wave of her arm. I wondered how she was put together, and if I could disconnect that arm.

She then directed me to the next phase of my orientation; a room called *Universe Geography*, and said she would return at the end of this lecture. I saluted her and watched her fluorescent green hair bounce as she walked away. It was then I decided I would have to give her some time-consuming 'errands' to send her on.

This was a smaller room with nothing but an odd-looking chair floating in the middle of it. The chair had an almost human–like spine for its back and a very plush purple seat. When I sat down in it, it slowly tilted back so that I was facing the ceiling. The ceiling then retracted, revealing the universe as seen from Zio with the naked eye. My chair began moving higher and higher until I felt as if I was out among the stars and planets. Maybe I was. Stranger things had happened here so far.

Another Ziot made his entrance, floating horizontally about six feet above my head. He expressed his concern for my safety.

"You mean it's okay for me to travel through space in my sleep, but you're concerned I might fall out of my chair to the floor?" The Ziot smiled. He pointed with his long, thin finger to my seat belt. I buckled up, smiling back.

I saw Earth for the first time from this planet, and its relation to the rest of this superuniverse, as it was being referred to in the lecture. It was very clear that the real name for Earth is Urantia. There were seven superuniverses from what I understood so far, and only a fraction of the universe where Urantia was located was inhabited. I couldn't imagine the size of the rest of the universe if this was true.

I decided to ask a question. "Sir, I need something clarified. Are Ziots physical or spiritual beings?"

"We are *Ophanim*," he responded. "We are spiritual, but can take material form. The ranking of different entities spiral outward from the center of His presence, the Divine Source of Light and Love. There are three main divisions: *Seraphim*, *Cherubim*, and *Ophanim*. Ophanim inhabit the outer region, which begins to take form and substance nearest Urantia. Our ruler is Gabriel, the female Archangel, as you call her."

"Why are you depicted with wings on our planet if you are Ophanim?" I asked.

The Ziot continued, "Human beings have sometimes been permitted to observe Seraphim or other entities who inhabit these spiraling regions which are being prepared for transport service. They were observed as they prepared to receive a passenger for interplanetary transit. In reality, these wings are energy insulators – friction shields."

"What about Guardian Angels," I asked? "Do they really exist?"

"Yes. There are sets of two Seraphim from a lower level of consciousness appointed to every physical human, and they remain with them until they reach the *morantia*, a higher level of spiritual awareness. They become very attached, too. They care deeply for the humans they watch over and are with them when the records are revealed. They never leave their side. Seraphim experience deep emotions and cry over one particular thing often … the fear and anxiety humans possess. It is so unnecessary and saddens them deeply, but they understand it is due to the offspring of Adam and Eve mixing with the lower breeds who inhabited Urantia.

"The first two humans placed on Urantia were given free will to either follow our Creator or follow the fallen angels. After making their decision to follow the high-ranking Seraphim and his followers who had turned away from the Creator, they began breeding with the lower forms of life living on the planet. This brought fear to them as they began to experience pain, sickness, death, and other negativities. Guardian angels are sympathetic and affectionate, but non-sexual."

My thoughts and imagination were racing to keep up with this information. I was afraid I wouldn't be able to digest everything I was being told. The Ziot felt this and said, "You must get rid of fear. We will work with you on this. Trust us. I want you to pay very close attention to the history of the fallen angels. You can study this in your room if you wish. It will be the focus of your orientation and your means to understanding many things before you continue here on Zio."

The Ziot abruptly ascended and exited horizontally, the same way he had entered. I knew he was right and this was all the information I could handle for now. My mind was racing and I wondered what the fallen angels had to do with me. I was beginning to trust the Ziots' judgment and decided to let it go for now. After all, they were much more intelligent and advanced than I was.

I was becoming attuned to Amie's timing and just as I began to anticipate her appearance, she in fact, appeared. Standing in front of me she explained, "I believe your orientation will resume tomorrow beginning with the history of Urantia. I've been instructed to inform you that you should take the rest of the day off from learning, and begin again with your evening gardening duties. Would you like to prepare for the next tour of Zio, taking place in one hour, Urantia time?"

It sounded interesting and fun. "Sure," I replied.

JOANNE JOHNSON

# 4. THE TOUR

I LOOKED FORWARD TO EXPLORING ZIO further. Later I could contact Hank on my mega media system. I had some questions I was sure he could answer. If I had any difficulty operating it, Amie would come out of the wall to help me. That android was something else. I wondered if she spied on me all night long or if she was activated by the sound of my voice and remained in the wall in the 'off' position. I thought of her as a 'green machine,' her hair symbolic of her recycled parts and energy-saving mechanisms.

When I passed through my door and the orange mist, she was waiting with my leaping shoes. The mist kept me feeling so good all the time now, I didn't remember feeling any other way.

There she stood, ready to serve, anticipating my every need.

I thanked her, but wished she would let me do some things for myself. I decided to save that comment for later. I was fully aware that we would be leaving the safe zone and she was necessary. I had no idea what to expect and was both nervous and excited about the tour.

She made that same polite gesture with her arm, so I followed her down an unfamiliar hall that led to another corridor. I could hear a high-pitched beep that got louder as we approached two large metal doors. An android, male in appearance, with orange fluorescent hair and a silver two-piece service uniform, stood at the door distributing equipment to everyone who approached. Amie received a very large weapon and I got a quickly placed helmet on my head. It fastened automatically under my chin with a loud click. I checked to see if there had been any damage done, but my chin and neck felt intact. From what I had noticed, the helmet was the same shape as our skulls, and was made out of a chalky white material, giving us all an eerie appearance. Amie led the way into a white, oddly round-shaped aircraft floating just outside the door. It rocked only slightly while suspended in the air.

The passengers already seated were humans like myself. They faced the windows with their backs to the interior of the craft. I sat down next to a man who said hello with a thick Italian accent. He seemed friendly, so I responded with a smile. I did a quick survey and saw happy, chatty people anticipating a positive and eventful tour. This helped me relax... a little. After buckling up, our seats reclined and I felt a slight giration accompanied by a soft 'swoosh' sound. The caft was slowly moving upward, from what I could tell. I felt the push of g-force on my body for about three seconds. Our seats returned to the upward position and my mouth fell open. We were now traveling sideways at an incredibly high velocity. The Italian man was enjoying my reaction. This was obviously not his first tour.

The vehicle suddenly stopped and hovered over a bright red, flat desert area. Odd-looking rock formations that resembled triple-decker ice cream cones stood clustered on the sand. They appeared smooth and round with each protrusion getting smaller towards the top. Vivid colors of purple, teal, and green seem to radiate from these rock clusters.

As we landed, I noticed several large birds with fancy tails prancing about. They strutted as if they ejoyed having an audience. A four-legged mammal, slightly resembling a rabbit, perked up his tall, long ears from behind a rock and bounced away. This was about the strangest looking creature I had ever encountered. It had three skinny legs, a fat body, and bulging eyes. Its mouth was flat and round, like someone had made the letter 'O' out of black silly putty and slapped it on its face. The bird-like creatures made clucking sounds. They took flight and dove at the mammal, and he was snatched up by the skin on his back. They all feasted on him in the air, pulling his flesh away quickly and ravenously. I saw his bones drop to the ground, the meal completed in about four seconds.

"Well that was nice," I thought. I certainly didn't want to get out here, but that's exactly what we did. 'So this is what they feed us to?' I wondered.

Amie walked beside me as we exited down a ramp. I wondered where the birds had gone and kept an eye upward. Amie and the other androids checked small square objects strapped to their wrists. They resembled large watches with video screens. Maybe the objects helped the androids check the skies, too.

The other people were enjoying the tour and smiling. I was sure it was scheduled frequently and was meant to be enjoyable. I knew the androids were highly competent or the Orphanim wouldn't trust our safety to them. I began to relax and admired the beautiful rock formations. They glistened with an almost dripping clear substance and vibrated with soft musical tones as we approached. The others were touching them. When I did this, a feeling of peace overcame me and a surge went through my body that left me feeling extremely refreshed and mellow. 'It was even legal and free,' I thought. I rubbed a second rock of brilliant teal color and was feeling quite good when I heard a siren. I looked anxiously at Amie and saw her staring intently at the watch–like monitor on her arm. She then took her long ray gun and pointed it up at the sky. My worst fear became reality as one of the enormous birds appeared over us flapping its multi-colored wings. I heard the others scream, but Amie destroyed the bird quickly and it dispersed colorfully into a million pieces. She checked her video-watch and said it was now safe to continue. We walked about a mile more, rubbing and enjoying the rock formations.

When we finally returned to the transport vessel, I took a better look at it. It was shaped like a wheel. We had been sitting in a large circle facing outward. There was a small raised cubicle at the center of the wheel. There sat the pilot. It was not an android. It was something else, resembling a metallic octopus. This steel-like robot operated the vehicle we were transported in with its many tentacles. I could also see two androids checking on things in the cubicle so I assumed they had it all under control.

We flew on for about an hour, covering a vast stretch of land. As we moved, the sky began to darken, and I guessed we were on the other side of the planet. The aircraft stopped abruptly and slowly descended into a beautiful complex with white structures and soft lights. Strange looking trees swayed gracefully. They resembled palm trees in varying shades of pink with tentacle-like branches.

An announcement informed us that we would now visit "The luminous ones from *Vantis*." Amie kept some distance from me. I presumed this was because this was a safe place.

We gathered at the base of some steps which led up to a majestic edifice with tall columns and no roof. In fact, now that I was closer, I noticed that none of the buildings had roofs. Then, they appeared. Beautiful humanoids filled with light descended the steps. They had an almost glowing, albino appearance. Their eyes shone with a piercing violet brilliance. They were very calm and gracious, moving slowly as they bowed their heads to greet us. Their bodies only slightly varied from ours. They were much taller, thin in stature, not very muscular. They were hairless. Their thin, almost completely transparent one-piece tunics gently moved in the breeze. I couldn't tell their sex and guessed they were all the same.

A woman next to me said, "Aren't they beautiful?"

"Why are they here?" I asked her.

"Oh, they're here temporarily to act as intercessors for Urantia and two other planets of the seven super-universes that are about to enter a new age, a higher state of consciousness. Soon, on our home planet, they will share advanced revelations about spirituality and Our Creator. These teachings will be understood and shared by everyone through collective consciousness after humans make their transition. The luminous beings are starting to be seen everywhere on our home planet in the sky and near the ground. They are very loving and kind. They can travel throughout the universe, and don't need any vehicle."

The luminous humanoids waved and left. We climbed the steps and entered an open area where a feast was displayed on a table.

Everyone sampled what seemed to be a vegetarian buffet. There were nuts, fruit, and a large variety of breads and biscuits included. Water in golden goblets was available for us to drink. I asked a young woman if this is what they ate here, but she said this was her first tour and she was wondering the same thing. I looked for Amie. She had moved closer since I'd entered the building. I felt pretty sure now that she was programmed to maintain about a thirty yard visual on me under normal circumstances.

I approached her, asking her if the luminous ones ate a vegetarian diet and she responded, "The Vantis population no longer has need for food."

"Oh, I see," I responded. Next I asked, "Are the humans from Earth, I mean, Urantia, at the bottom of the scale of universal evolution?"

"I would say you are in the middle," Amie said.

"What are the lowest forms of humanoids like, then?"

She then said something I never would have imagined possible. "They are one brained, mid-breathers due to their atmosphere, and very forgetful. Therefore, they cannot organize themselves or accomplish much. They just sit around and eat."

"Thanks, Amie," I said. I detected a slight note of superiority injected into her previous answer.

When I asked her about androids and their place in the progress of evolution, she gave an unemotional answer. "We are neither evolving nor spiritually progressing. We are a product of the highly intelligent species of *Nebadon*, the three-brained humanoids from one of the more central superuniverses. They assist on special projects like this one on Zio."

"Thanks, Amie," I said again. I still thought I noticed a slight 'feeling' injected in her description of the lowest humanoids.

I reminded myself to ask Hank later that night what project on Zio she was referring to.

After lunch, our tour proceeded to one of the adjacent buildings. Two androids took turns narrating as we walked through a white, dimly lit building. There were many large books on pedestals inside. They were encased in illuminated clear stands and bore symbols which indicated the names of planets, most of which I had never heard of. The Book of Urantia was pointed out to us. It had a glowing indigo cover resembling acrylic or glass with silver symbols embossed on it. This building held the history of each planet as it progressed in higher stages of consciousness and spiritualism. The color of each book corresponded to the color of the first race on each planet. There were three black, non-illuminated ones against a wall farther away. I asked one of the androids about them and he said they were planets distinguished from space and time. "You mean they are gone? Non-existent?" I asked.

"Yes, that is correct," he responded. I was afraid to ask what had happened to them.

We returned to the transport already hovering slightly above the ground. Some of the passengers settled in and listened to harmonics and various other types of music with a tiny device inserted into their ear. Others read additional information about Zio and the surrounding planets using a pair of dark tinted glasses. The information was contained in the lenses. The information could then be scrolled using your fingertips on small dials located on the side of the glasses. The use of these 'recreational travel tools' had been explained by an android just before our initial departure. There had been no safety precautions discussed. I presumed travel in this manner was either safe, or resulted in a crash at speeds that didn't leave any survivors.

Deciding that some music would help me put that thought out of my head quickly, I inserted one of the little music devices in my ear, and turned on by blinking my eyes twice. I reclined my seat and let the music and the craft carry me away.

# 5. CALIGASTIA

THE TRANSPORT VEHICLE RETURNED US to our dwellings on the other side of the planet, and finally I realized we hadn't used our leaping shoes. I turned to Amie, my ever-present shadow, and asked her why. She said it was because the *Slavas* were hibernating early. I didn't pursue this. I was tired of the sound of her monotone, mechanical voice.

I went straight to the massive garden to get my duties over with, anxious to return to my room. I had many questions for Hank and research to do. Following the instructions posted on the garden entrance, I washed my hands in a purple solution and put on a pair of thin gloves made out of a pink skin-like material. They sparkled with tiny lights running all over them in intricate patterns. A man with light brown hair and a distinct

German accent, who appeared to be in his twenties, told me that the gloves were illuminated with electro-magnetic pulses that detected contamination from outside germs and that if the gloves turned red I must throw them away and get a fresh pair. I pulled weeds, watered, and carried ripe vegetables and fruits in red crates to a belt that carted them off somewhere. The crates were extremely lightweight and seemed to make the produce lighter than normal to carry. There was a seed bank in a separate room from the assigned area of the garden. These had been gathered, dried, and packaged with labels. The German man went on to tell me that everything was organic. There were no pesticides or chemicals needed. The ecosystem here was perfect, and kept free of invading pests or diseases. I enjoyed handling the familiar vegetables from my homeland.

Once in my room, I closed the door behind me, kicked my shoes off, and dropped the rest of my clothes on the closet floor. It felt good to have some privacy. I walked through the bathroom with the large Jacuzzi pool and turned right to the last unexplored room where I found a large rain forest type shower. I stepped into it and found myself pleasantly surrounded on three sides by exotic foliage. I wanted to turn the water on, but saw no dial or faucet. (I was pretty sure it was a shower.) I sure didn't want Amie to appear during my private relaxation time, so I hurried to try to figure it out. I cautiously reached into the plants and felt a solid wall, almost elbow deep in to the foliage. I retracted fom the wall and as I reached upward a light rain shower began to fall. Thank goodness! I waved my hand over my head again and the water adjusted to a heavier stream.

I forgot soap! Dripping wet, I stepped outside the shower and began looking for it. An area on the opposite wall had a soft amber glow about one foot in diameter shining through its surface. I put my hand on it and the wall opened to reveal three shelves with a generous supply of luxurious lotions, soaps, and personal hygiene products. This was turning out to be the icing on the cake to my day so far. I looked around and noted there wasn't much more in the room. Maybe there was, but I didn't want to take the time to play 'what's behind door number 1, 2, or 3'. I had noticed a disc-shaped area on the floor just outside the shower and was pretty sure it was used to dry off. There was another one in the room with the pool. I stood on it after showering and it rotated slowly while air blew from the wall drying me from head to toe. I grabbed a soft, loose-fitting beige garment that resembled a nightgown. It would do. I was beginning to feel normal again.

I sat down at the floating chair and tried to decipher the keyboard. I discovered that I was lucky enough to figure out how to turn it on, as the media wall to lit up and moved closer. The names of about twenty planets, including Urantia, were located on one side of the keyboard. It would be fun to explore those planets and their life forms later on. I pressed Urantia and immediately saw Earth on the screen. I was doing pretty good on my own so far. Now, how do I reach Hank? I engaged something that indicated size but it zoomed into the wrong country, India. Next, I located the place to run a search, and typed Dulce, NM, USA. I then put my hand up to the the map and with my fingertips, zoned in on Hank's street and found the RV and the yard with his recycled art. That was easy!

Suddenly, I heard a familiar voice. "Greetings. How do you like Zio?"

"Is that you, Hank?" I asked.

"Yep. So, how are things going?"

"Not bad. How do I begin a video chat, Hank?"

"Ask it whatever you want. You've gotten this far, the rest is easy."

"Show me Hank," I said. Suddenly, there he was before me, in a pair of overalls and no shirt, sitting at his kitchen table. Not the most flattering attire, with his bony, hairy arms showing. "What's that you're eating, a frozen dinner?" I asked him.

"Yep, it's meatloaf - my favorite."

"Why don't you take better care of yourself?"

"Don't have time. There's a planet to the north trying to interfere with Earth's magnetic field. Those damn *Hegronites* are the most evil little bastards I've ever encountered." He took a bite of meatloaf. "What are you up to? Have you finished your orientation?"

"No. I'm supposed to do research on the fallen angels."

"Now there's an interesting subject. Pay attention to what you learn about the Seraphim, *Lucifer*, who thought he knew more than our Creator. Lucifer is a brilliant being of light. Never met the fellow, of course. He didn't agree with some of our Creator's plans concerning the beginning of intelligent life on Urantia. He stirred up a little trouble, but it was the legion of entities led by Satan that really defected and turned rebel. They claimed Urantia as theirs, but were cast away by the Archangel Michael. Some went off into the universe and corrupted other planets and others remained mating with the daughters of men and eventually going underground, literally. Those damn little Hegronites are a mutation of Satan's race.

"When you're researching, pay attention to the Nebadons as well. They are our allies."

"I've heard of them. They're seven feet tall, three brained and more advanced than us?"

"Yep, that's them."

Everything started getting garbled and I could barely hear Hank say, "Gotta go. We've got a nosy *Dackhart* trying to listen in on us." Then he was gone. I would try to ask him more questions another time. Maybe he wouldn't be so busy tomorrow.

I was on my own again and still on the subject of Urantia so I blurted out "fallen angels." A life-size, tall male suddenly appeared in front of me as a hologram. It frightened me. I gasped, falling backwards to the floor and felt foolish lying there looking up at the ceiling. I looked at the hollogram again. It was still there - a male clothed in a red and gold satin robe with thick wavy hair touching his shoulders. He had a demeanor suggesting royalty accustomed to leading. He looked so real! Do I ask him a question? Do I want to? "Who are you?" I finally asked.

I am *Caligastia*, the fallen Prince of Urantia. I proclaimed myself absolute sovereign ruler of this planet 50,000 years ago, the same time that the six-colored or Sangik races appeared there."

I sat back down and gathered mysef again. "Can you tell me the history of Urantia at that time and your connection with the fallen angels?"

He moved closer. He was facing me now and I felt threatened. I had to remind myself he was only a hologram, an effective informational tool at most.

He continued, "I arrived with a group of one hundred volunteer ascending beings to establish my headquarters in Mesopotamia, the center of the world population at that time. Ascending beings act as advisors and helpers sent by God to carry out early race improvement on all young worlds. I led a corps of one hundred such helpers.

"We are invisible to mortals. You are viewing only a representation of me, as no mortal being has ever seen our kind. On Urantia, the plans for planetary progress and cultural advancement were well under way, when the whole enterprise was brought to a rather sudden end by my adherence to the Lucifer rebellion."

"How did life begin on Urantia?" He turned slightly, looking at me over his left shoulder. He seemed to be a proud, intelligent and rather forceful being. He began speaking again.

"When Earth became stable and acceptable for the development of life, members of the *Life Carrier Corps* were sent to determine the life forms most suitable to inhabit the planet. They conducted more than half a million experiments before deciding on a pattern of life. About five hundred million years ago, the Life Carriers planted life in three locations in the shallows of the ocean that coverd Urantia. Life did not evolve slowly. New orders of life appear suddenly, contrary to the modern conclusions of your scientists. They had projected a sodium chloride pattern of life. The Urantia protoplasm can function only in a suitable salt solution. All vegetable and animal life evolved in this solution. Urantia life, however, is unique. There is no other world that has life just like that of Urantia. All life up to my time on Urantia as Planetary Prince had origin in marine life. With the expected emergence of land, land life emerged. The Life Carriers were finally able to see the results of their efforts when the first human beings appeared among the stock of progressing primates. The first human beings were Andon and Fonta who beget the Sangik children. Among these nineteen children were five red, four yellow, four blue, two indigo, two orange, and two green."

"The development of the first human family was an eventful

and exciting day with the beginning of mind, will, and dignity on Urantia.

"I might add, that since life was established on Urantia, the Life Carriers have improved healing techniques and introduced them on another world. They offer more pain relief and better means to cure one's self of disease.

I needed a break. This was a lot of information and none of it was even slightly familiar. I pressed the pause button and walked away from the keyboard. The prince was beginning to be comfortable company. I looked back at him standing there motionless. I liked this method of learning. I also liked the control it offered me.

I stepped closer to the transparent exterior wall. The sky was magnificent here on Zio. I could see the moon rising, still very large in appearance. I watched it change colors as it made its way across the sky and tried to process the information I was receiving. Was it true that Urantia life was an experiment by extraterrestrials? Was material life only a temporary biological existence to experience in order to progress to a higher morantia plane until we gain our eternal home? Was this what mortal life was all about? If this was so, then there were other entities very involved in our existence, and spiritual beings were everywhere. Why couldn't we see them?

I returned to the keyboard and pressed play. Caligastia continued his lecture telling me that there were two hundred *Watchers* (sons of God) assisting the seven archangels in the creation of Eden. "During that time these Watchers taught men some of the arts of civilization. The trouble was that their more recreational activities included the unexpected seduction of the daughters of Andon. The angels who followed Lucifer, were attracted to the harlots, the painted ones who flaunted their bodies. They were easily seduced. They were angels, but were vulnerable because they transformed upon contact with earth and turned into flesh. These angels were later referred to as the gigantic *Gregori*.

"Lucifer was guilty of 'hubris'—translated as pride—but its real meaning was sexual passion. This highly powerful angel was said to have been the Highest Angel, second only to God himself. There was a mighty war in the universe between these good and evil spiritual beings. That's when Michael, the great Archangel, chased the evil spirits out of Urantia to be cast in many directions into all the other universes. Lucifer has since repented and been absolved of his sins. He remains a great being of light, very high in the ranks of angels.

"In closing, I will tell you one thing more. Some of the fallen angels hid under the surface of Urantia, and remain there waiting for Satan to return to claim the planet. Satan was one of Lucifer's most powerful leaders and to this day his hordes remain loyal to him, rather than turn to the Light. This confirms they are either stupid, proud, stubborn, or just follow their own dark motives."

Prince Caligastia was suddenly motionless. I presumed this was the end of his lecture.

I returned the hologram to the wall and turned it off. The floating bed with the transparent mattress was calling my name. I waved my hand toward the ceiling and the lights turned off. My brain was filled with so much new information that I feared I would be up all night thinking about it all. "No, don't worry about it." I decided out loud. What I really wanted to know about was the project on Zio Amie was referring to. Were we all another extraterrestrial experiment here on Zio? I fell into a well-deserved sleep.

# 6. COME FLY WITH ME

THE NEXT MORNING, I changed into a pale green dress and noticed the clothes I had left on the floor yesterday had been picked up. I hadn't asked Amie to do this for me.

I headed towards the dining room for breakfast, and as I walked, my eye caught glimmers from me dress. Sometimes it would give off a small sparkle, sometimes a bright light. I enjoyed watching it shimmer as I moved. This was my first time wearing an 'interactive garment' and I wondered if it had a purpose other than sheer entertainment.

As I entered the dining room, what I saw next almost sent me screaming all the way back to my room. Instead, I took a deep breath, tried to compose myself, and choose a seat close to the door. Then very slowly I looked around to the two unusual extraterrestrials seated at a nearby table. Everyone was acting normal except for a woman who had said she was on her first tour yesterday. She looked paralyzed and had a wide-eyed, unblinking expression that spelled complete terror. I found this comforting, because I felt the same way.

One of the creatures was a humanoid with an elongated cranial structure that swept about two feet upward, and curved toward the back of its head. The chest was heavily protruded, resembling a medieval warrior's breastplate, only it was part of his body. It moved as he breathed. His skin was thick and coarse like that of an elephant or rhinoceros. He began to make very deep vibrating sounds. This startled me and I accidentally knocked my glass of 'green muck' over on the table.

The other creature looked like a child's birthday party balloon animal. Interestingly enough, he was also humanoid. He had two eyes, two holes for a nose, a slit for a mouth, as well as four appendages, from what I could see. There was an opaque film surrounding him, making it difficult to see his features clearly. A green gas also surrounded him.

The 'balloon person' spoke to the 'pointed-head person' in a squeaky high-pitched language that grated on me. I then realized the deep vibrating sounds I had heard were a form of communication. Amazing! They actually understood each other.

Suddenly, the pointed-head person turned and looked at me, extending one of his birdlike claws towards my spilled drink. I froze! Had I been staring? I didn't know if he wanted to speak to me or eat me, and I certainly hoped I hadn't offended him.

Just then, a Ziot entered the dining room from an unknown location and the room became very quiet. He raised one hand, facing everyone in a salutation. He greeted our temporary visitors and explained that they were here for the day while androids repaired their spacecraft. They were on a mission from one of the six concentric ellipses, the space levels encircling the central isle. This I did not understand. He also added that they were quite advanced and friendly. This was probably the most welcome explanation for our earthly ears. The 'balloon person' stood up and squeaked several times. The Ziot nodded in agreement adding that it is always a gratifying experience for peaceful space bothers to meet one another. He continued by saying that he hoped they would be comfortable here and must always know that they are welcome on Zio.

What I wanted to know was exactly where they would be sleeping if they stayed overnight, and if it would be far away from my room.

Still feeling somewhat confused by this new encounter with material beings from another world, I thought I had handled it rather well, overall. I based this on the dazed and frightful expression of the other newcomer which still hadn't changed. I wondered if they ever sent humans back to Earth.

I finished my cereal and left, going back to the orientation hall, to the Universe Geography room. After I sat in the purple chair, the Ziot instructor floated in again and descended in front of me. He related that he was pleased with my progress on the study of the fallen angels, and he would proceed with more geography today. I wouldn't have been surprised if my personal time was monitored, but perhaps knowing things without being present to see them unfold was typical of spiritual beings.

My seat once again slowly lifted up towards the stars on the ceiling until I felt as if I was out in space. "Do you see that very large spiral of clustered stars and planets?" he asked.

"I do."

"That is Nebadon. It is in a superuniverse that is much

older than yours. The inhabitants have not only balanced their environment to control weather and other natural phenomena, but they have advanced spiritually at the same rate of speed. They are dedicated to the harmonious balance of life and their planet while maintaining their devotion to The Creator. He is first with them and they are very aware He is the source of everything. There is no crime, physical defects or illness any longer there.

All the inhabited planets of this cluster of planets cooperate with each other. Nebadon is the name of the very large central orange planet in this cluster, the other planets surrounding it have no names, only numbers.

Nebadon life expectancy is 400 years. The beings there are three brained, unlike Urantians who have a left and right side making them two brained. Nebadons have cultivated their psychic abilities to no longer need speech to communicate. Over time, we've been speaking to you more and more telepathically. Have you noticed that since you have been here?"

My head reeled and I felt faint with the realization of this hitting just now. Everything had been happening so fast; it was the least important thing to dwell on.

"Exactly," he said. "You have been filled with unfamiliar sensations and you have had to rely on your innate skills.

"Today, if it pleases you, it would be good to focus more on the history of the fallen angels and the existence of the seven superuniverses." He continued his lesson. "Each superuniverse is simply a section of space that makes up approximately one seventh of the organized and partially inhabited material creation. Your local universe is one of the newer creations in Orvonton, the seventh superuniverse. Although Nebadon is much older than your world, it is considered to be in a relatively new universe." I was confused. Maybe I could get Hank to explain it to me later tonight.

He continued, "Your local universe holds its existence as part of this magnificent genesis in the outer limits of organized and inhabited creation, near the outer border, in a far off corner. Your world is called Urantia, number 606 in the planetary group. This system has 619 inhabited worlds, and more than 200 additional planets are evolving favorably toward becoming inhabited worlds at some future time.

"Now I would like to quote from The Book of Urantia, your reference for understanding who you are and your connection to spiritual and material existence on your planet. It was written as a guide for your home planet by one of our very own Ziots.

> *'He shall send his angels and they shall gather*
> *together his elect from the four winds.'*
> The inhabited Worlds 568:8

He then turned and looked at me in silence. I almost lost consciousness looking into his huge black eyes and as I went deeper into their darkness, I felt compassion and love as he gazed back at me.

A huge burden was being laid upon me, expectations I didn't understand. I was being made accountable for something and being challenged to question the purpose of my very existence. This was way over my head. All I've done until now was pay my bills and try to be fairly hospitable to my fellow man.

He slowly drifted upward.

As I left the Universe Geography room, Amie intercepted me and instructed me to follow her to a meditation gathering where I could socialize afterwards. We proceeded toward a group of about ten people who had gathered near the door. Amie told me this was my assigned group meditation time. She said I was free to join whenever I wanted to. A bell softly chimed, notifying us it was time to enter.

"Thank you for picking up my clothes," I said. "It was very thoughtful of you." Amie smiled. I continued, "If there is anything I can ever do for you, just ask me, Amie." I watched her walk off in her usual perky gait with her fluorescent green hair bouncing up and down. She turned and looked back at me and then went on her way.

SHE HAD SMILED! I knew she had feelings. I just knew it. I had read before coming here, that scientists would one day invent androids that not only looked uncannily human but also possessed feelings, reacting with emotions to certain events. It will challenge us when robots step too far towards being humanlike It will be something our brains have difficulty assimilating. Maybe this was why the androids here didn't want us to know much about them, making things simpler for us. I would guard my new secret wisely.

I hurried into the mediation room to catch up with the others. Despite the breakthrough with Amie, I still felt very burdened and somewhat depressed from my last lecture. I didn't see mats anywhere for sitting on the floor and meditating. Everyone just stood there waiting for something to happen. Chanting began, similar to the deep-throat singing of Tibetan monks. It was mixed with an unknown musical instrument that sounded like running one's finger around the rim of a glass of water, only softer. The entire experience was soothing and yet strange.

The ceiling retracted, revealing the sky. Everyone looked up and as I followed their gaze, I saw about ten Ziots slowly descending. It was quite a sight to see so many together with their eyes glowing fluorescent yellow and their arms crossed over their chests. They each floated down to one of us and when I was approached, I understood the Ziot to tell me to relax and not be afraid. He took my hands and I felt a jolt go through my body. I looked into his large eyes and felt my body rise slowly higher and higher. Before I reazlied what had happened, I found myself flying on my own, next to him. I looked down and saw canyons, deserts, forests, and finally the ocean. Zio isn't so different from Earth, I thought. I began seeing houses, cities, railroads and industry. At the sight of these things that were so familiar to me, I felt disoriented and confused, and began to fall, screaming wildly, tumbling over and over. Everything slowed down as I felt his hand take mine again. Then our journey continued, with me flying next to him, holding his hand for security.

"Wait! Were we on Earth or Zio?"

I heard the Ziot say, "You are on your home planet, Urantia." I didn't understand how we had gotten here so fast. I knew about quantum leaping from a dream, but I was awake. He informed me that using time portals to travel through time and space would become second nature to me. "You have already traveled faster than light to Zio many times in your sleep because you used your subconscious to release this ability, even though you do not yet understand it consciously. Just relax. This will come easier the more you do it."

In a blink of an eye, we were back in the meditation room. My flying partner was already ascending with the other Ziots. They certainly don't give you time to become attached, I thought. They were very purposeful beings, however, and I had the highest regard for them.

Only humans remained in the room and they assembled in a circle holding hands. I joined in and waited for something to happen. Nothing did.

Sheesh, I thought, I am not overly fond of the silly rituals of transcendental meditation. The mantras are ridiculous little syllables that are a simple mental repetition of words. I had also heard that advanced technique focused on parts of the body, the environment, the world and even outer space. Naah! I already knew nothing was going to happen and frankly I could think of a lot of other things I would rather be doing.

Oh! What was that? I felt faint vibrations passing through my body. It made me terribly nervous and the need to flee took over. I looked around wondering what or who was responsible. Everyone had their eyes closed so I decided to close mine, too, and wait for the whole thing to be over. The vibration got stronger. This was even without a mantra. The group remained still for about three minutes and finally the vibrations ended. I had to admit, I was very refreshed and my mind was sharp and clear. The circle dispersed and everyone went on about their business as if nothing had happened.

I walked over to an oriental woman with beautiful, long, jet-black hair. She greeted me with a hug and said, "Welcome." I introduced myself and asked her about the vibrations.

She said, "We send out vibrations on a higher level of consciousness than transcendental meditation. You will soon master it." I wondered how many years she considered 'soon.'

"You must pray for your home planet and concentrate positive energy to help it. You will realize when your mental state changes and you, too, can send out vibrations for healing and change."

"But, I felt vibrations coming *into* my body. Was that

normal?"

"Actually, we were sending them to you because you are new here and need to develop your skills."

"Why is everyone telling me that? Why do I need to develop anything at all? Are we all part of some project here?"

She smiled and assured me I would understand in time. She said I was doing fine and it would all unfold as it should and couldn't be rushed.

Her Chinese name was Ting, meaning 'graceful.' She invited me to her room and we chatted on the way. Her room was an exact replica of mine. I asked her what she studied in the evenings and told me dysmorphology. She said she typically did research to identify environmental causes of birth defects.

A soft bell chimed. I guessed it was time for lunch, and Ting confirmed. On the way to the dining room, I asked her if the frightening beings who appeared at breakfast would also be having lunch with us, but she said they had left as soon as their spacecraft had been repaired.

She looked at me with a whimsical expression and laughed, her dark, slanted eyes smiling. "Was that your first encounter?" she asked.

"No, I am getting kinda used to being shocked." I smiled and felt very pleased.

JOANNE JOHNSON

# 7. ESCAPE TO NEBADON

I CONTINUED MY DAY after lunch with Ting, and the occasional conversations with others, doing some research on The Book of Urantia and then attending to my evening gardening duties. One thing I had noticed so far was that everyone here was very devoted to scientific or medical research. This dedication was obvious in the amount of lab time they indulged in daily. I was beginning to feel out of place, although I realized some of the others had been here seventy or even ninety years longer than me. That's plenty of time to cultivate a specialty and become quite successful in making astounding discoveries.

I sat down at my media wall and called on Hank after getting settled back in my room. He was doing nothing and I was glad. "So how are you, Hank?"

"Oh, I'm my usual cranky, unpleasant self. The real question is how are you?"

"How did you know? I'm confused. I don't understand why I'm here."

"You're there for a reason, missy. Believe me, it's an important one or you wouldn't be there. You'll just have to figure that one out for yourself."

"Well, can you explain in a way that I can understand it where the superuniverses are located in relation to our own material universe?"

"Sure, I can try. The zoning of the master universe in association with the alternate clockwise and counterclockwise flow of the galaxies is a factor in the stabilization of physical gravity, designed to prevent the accentuation of gravity pressure from reaching the point of disruptive activities. You see, such an arrangement exerts antigravity influence and acts as a brake upon otherwise dangerous velocities."

"Okay, I'm with you so far, I think."

"The final proof of both a circular universe and delimited universe is afforded to us by the well known fact that all forms of basic energy swing around a curved path of space in obedience to the absolute pull of Paradise gravity. Does that make sense to you?"

"Yes. I'm still with you."

"Now, the zones between the space levels, such as the ones separating the seven superuniverses from eacho other and from the outer space level, are enormous elliptical regions of quiescent space activities. These zones also separate the vast galaxies racing around Paradise in orderly procession. Still with me?"

"I think so, Hank. I just never dreamt that there was so

much life out there, so many different spiritual, material, and partially material beings."

"Well, you have to recognize a balance and see that there is good and evil in all things, the positive and the negative existing at the same time. Nothing can exist without that. You have to acknowledge that there are good entities and bad, just as there are good and bad humans."

He continued, "I've been contemplating is the physics of the future and how we personally affect things just by thinking about them, for example. The true nature of molecules, atomic and subatomic particles, is completely different than what modern science has been able to discover. With future physics, we will learn how vital we are to everything around us. This new knowledge will enlighten us to our role in creation, the responsibility we have to eachother, and make us more 'God-like' than we ever imagined possible. I eagerly anticipate the new era about to begin on our planet. We're about to enter an age of superior knowledge and capabilities. I'm glad that I'm alive to witness it."

"What exactly is your job, Hank. Who are you?"

"I told you. I work with several species. I'm a retired physicist. I used to work for our government, in secret operations mostly connected to UFO occurrences. That was back when we began to become aware of them. I broke away from that due to a conflict in morals and personal ethics. I now represent the very entities who have visited our planet for centuries, as far back as ancient history. I am still loyal to our planet, but I now serve in a more diplomatic capacity with our space brothers and their various galaxy communities trying to keep peace.

"Getting back to the UFO occurrences here on earth, I still keep tabs on the underground complexes built long ago by another group of life forms who still operate them (once fallen angels), who are planning to take over our planet in the war of Armageddon.

"There are two main groups of aliens on Earth, the greys and the reptoids. A smaller group, the Nordics, are a very attractive species, tall, blonde with blue eyes. They are separate from the others. The greys are responsible for abductions, animal mutulations and creating half man half alien hybrids already placed in key positions in the world waiting to dominate the planet in time for the antichrist to appear. Their largest base is under our village, Dulce, New Mexico. They chose it wisely. It's a sleepy little town with a population of about 900. The center of this mega underground complex with extensive tunnels for transportation is Archuleta Mesa. Other bases are located underground in Colorado, Arizona, Utah, California, Canada and Brazil. A surprising amount of native American Indians have known of this as well and have seen their vehicles, UFOs, leaving their bases. Some have even witnessed them shape-shift into humans. I stay very busy observing the base in New Mexico. There are a handful of us placed in strategic locations around the world. We give up our identity as a prerequisite for this position so we cannot be traced or found. I am funded by a private corporation, ASTRA (The Alliance of Science and Technology Research in America) but hidden from our government. I answer to an additional 'boss' as well, but cannot disclose that identity at this time.

"Are you aware that we owe toxic clean up and waste removal from our atmosphere to two species occupying planets in a nearby galaxy?"

Reflecting on this a moment, I replied, "I guess anything is possible."

"They have been doing us huge favors for many years, but have no motive for contacting us just yet. They are peaceful. Now do you see the need for a diplomat to work with these vital allies? It's my job to keep them happy and safe from our own military and the media. I keep my profile very low and inconspicuous for that reason. What really keeps me busy is keeping tabs on our permanent underground residents. Enough about me. Lets move on to the history of the fallen angels.

"It was the *Nephilim*, divine beings from heaven, who came to earth, saw how beautiful the daughters of men were and took wives from among them. Their offspring were the *Annunaki*, meaning 'from heaven who came to earth'. They were giants in those days and had six fingers and six toes. These defects were cloned into the DNA of mankind later becoming dormant. I will explain more about DNA and cloning later."

"The Watchers are a guardian class of angels that were assigned to watch over the earth and protect mankind. These angels, the Annunaki, are the Watchers. They are divided into two groups, the *Enki* and *Enlil*. The Enki took form here on earth and are among the various aliens who operate underground. Our government has had to contract with them to keep them from taking over and destroying us. They produced our hybrid-alien race of Sumarians and Egyptians. They used the giant offspring to build the unexplained large statues, stonehenge, the pyramids, etc. The Enki still conduct abductions for experiments, impregnate women and finally produce their hybrids. Our government has kept this from public knowledge or mass hysteria would break out. The thing is they have mastered dematerialization, enabling them to walk through walls. There's really nothing we can do. They can change into human form at will. They are most concerned with global dominance and control within the Third Faction for the new World Order. The truth is, an alien or demonic invasion is coming and it isn't coming from outer space."

"Are we in end times, Hank?"

"Of course we are. We are in the end of this span of our evolution. When seven billion souls exist on earth it marks the end of an evolution era and a new one will begin. We will change into more advanced beings with collective consciousness once a certain order of events have taken place. The only thing that could get in the way of that is, of course, the entrance of the antichrist, a hybridization creature that is fully fallen angel and fully man—a bastard angelic incarnation. The antichrist will be Satan's seed: a Naphilim. All along, the abductions and human breeding experiments were to perfect the ultimate breed, half man and half alien to produce Satan incarnate in man. They have him now, waiting for his cue to appear on earth.

"As I said, Annunaki are the Watchers. They have two groups, the Enki and Enlil. I have just described for you one faction. Now, pay close attention to what I am about to tell you.

"The other faction of the Watchers (or Annunaki) are the Enlil. They play a role as protectors of earth. They hate the fallen angels, now aliens who work secretly beneath the earth. They themselves are descendants of these same fallen angles, but do not work for Satan and still believe it is their duty to protect the earth. They maintained supernatural powers, but are in human form now. Many of the Enlil were asleep and had to be awakened to their supernatural abilities enabling them to participate in Armagedon and protect mankind when the antichrist returns to take over this planet."

"I'm going to make a brash, wild conclusion, Hank, that you're telling me all this because the group of humans here on Zio are all descendants of Enlil. I also assume that the genes skip around even within families."

"Congratulations."

A loud siren broke my concentration. I hadn't heard this type of alarm before and panicked. Amie appeared grabbing my arm and rushing me out the door.

"What is it? Where are we going?"

Amie did not respond. She was intensely focused and began corresponding with someone in an unknown language. Then, she stopped in her tracks and changed directions running down a corridor to our left. I had trouble keeping up with her. What really convinced me of the urgency was when she suddenly scooped me up in her arms and darted down this corridor at an unbelievable speed. We passed through double steel doors to a platform that began descending faster and faster. It dropped for at least two miles. "Amie? Tell me what's going on!" I screamed. Her green hair was standing straight up, and her eyes began glowing bright red as we descended. She was all lit up in different colors racing around her and I wondered if she was going to explode.

A very small capsule was floating at the end of a ramp on the other side of the steel doors. It was shaped like a cone. A male android stood by its opening. He quickly assisted me into its seat. Amie strapped us both in and we began moving. There were no windows. "Where are we going? Amie. Tell me what's happening!"

"Nebadon," she responded. "Planet 346-2. We are not piloting this craft, they are. And we are about to enter a worm hole."

"I'm scared."

"Don't be. They are highly capable beings that can get you to safety or even put you back together if something happens. No need to worry. I will tell you when we arrive and then you must be put to sleep for transporting into their atmosphere. Once inside a domicile, the air will be adapted to your needs and they will be wearing adaptive equipment instead of us. It is very safe there."

"Amie, but why? Why is all this happening and why were we on Zio and not in the Nebadon's universe in the first place?"

"You ask a lot of questions." She smiled and went back to reading the monitor located on a panel in front of her. "Zio has an atmosphere exactly like earth. We're almost there. Be prepared for a bumpy ride as we reach the vortex at the end of the worm hole."

"Whatever! This is beginning to feel like a bad dream."

I was still very firghtened, but couldn't help noticing what a masterpiece this highly capable android was.

The spacecraft began to shake and then vibrate with growing intensity. I was now seeing in multiples. Amie's face was visible six times to each side. I wasn't sure where she was actually located any longer and it made me feel dizzy. I felt a soft mist or spray suddenly touch my face. I closed my eyes and began feeling like I was slipping into sleep or who knows what, maybe dying. I had nothing but disgust for the whole thing.

I wished that I was back on Earth when I heard a voice say, "Welcome to 346-2."

Lazily, I lifted my eyelids while stretching. Suddenly my memory kicked in and I jumped to a sitting position ready to fight or run. A voice behind me said, "You can run if you want, but why waste the energy? No one here will harm you and you'll probably just get lost."

I turned quickly but saw nothing.

"Down here. We're not as tall as Urantians. Just please don't step on me when you get off the table."

Was this a dream? Was I really looking at a Nebadon?

He was a tiny humanoid about three feet tall, dressed in a purple one-piece jumpsuit. His plump little face and rosy cheeks gave him a comical appearance. His white hair was very kinky and long, sticking out in all directions. The deep furrows across his forehead hinted at something entirely different. Perhaps this was a sign he was close to four hundred years old and had spent many of those years in research. I couldn't guess his age, because he looked old and yet like a baby at the same time. His golden eyes bulged like a frog, giving him a wide scope of peripheral vision. I wondered why he was inside a bubble.

"Yes, he said, "the bubble allows us the transformation we need to be in your atmosphere. We don't look too different on the other planets in this universe, just small variations."

I felt embarrassed, knowing he had read my thoughts. I didn't want to appear rude or ungrateful and I was actually very much in awe of this super intelligent Nebadon.

"How do you like Amie?" he asked. "She is one of our more advanced androids created with more capabilities than the previous models."

I was glad she was not present to hear him say this.

"I have much respect for Amie as a person, I responded sharply."

His eyes quickly darted at me. He knew I had found out his secret and quickly changed the subject.

"Forgive me for being so rude. Would you like something to drink, some refreshment? You must be a bit exhausted traveling through a worm hole for the first time, and then there was all that excitement back on Zio."

"Tea would be nice. Can I help you get it?"

"On no, just remain there and I'll get it for you."

He floated across the room in his bubble and got something from the wall and floated back. He carried the cup of tea in his hand, the clear bubble substance still surrounding his arm, hand and fingers. I took it from him and his arm retracted into the bubble. I wondered how long we would remain here and where everyone else was. The tea tasted good! It was very warm with a slight taste of ginger and something floral. A scene from Alice and Wonderland darted across my mind as some anxiety sneaked in.

"I do wish all of you didn't have so much fear to cope with. I think as you discover your full potential and gifts, you will feel much better about that," he said.

He had read my thoughts again and cointinued, "What happened on Zio was another attack from the planet *Vorta*. They are winged beings resembling black bats. They will harm you and steal your powers. The greatest war your planet has ever seen is about to take place on Urantia. You and the other Enlils will play an important part in defending it from these and the many other evil creatures planning to gain dominion there."

"What can I do?"

"You ask me this when you traveled several times from Urantia to Zio, a planet several light years away? Well, if you must know, look over there at that wall. Now push it away."

"How?"

You already know how to do this. You must only use your instincts. I closed my eyes and concentrated very hard on pushing the wall away. Nothing happened.

"You must be a *Taijiquan*; that's a phrase borrowed from your Chinese Tai Chi practices. It means, 'forceful fist'. Point to the wall and move it."

I extended my arm towards the wall and pointed to it. It slowly began moving backwards. I could not believe my eyes.

"Wasn't that fun?"

I wondered about this little man. Was he really so advanced?

"Okay, I think you have recovered from your sleep." he said. "You will be shown to your room where you may stay until the attack is contained by the android army on Zio. Amie will be back in touch with you shortly. Oh, and how does that phrase go on Urantia? Don't judge a book by its cover?"

He and his bubble started drifting down a corridor.

I said, "Thank you for the tea. It was very nice meeting you."

"Likewise, dearie. Now follow me and I'll show you to your room," he said.

I sat there in disbelief of all that had happened. The fact that we had not used speech to communicate wasn't even at the top of the list.

JOANNE JOHNSON

# 8. THE LAND OF OZ

I followed him a short distance down the corridor, until he pointed to a door, then he disappeared down another hallway, and slowly floated away. I opened the door and entered an amazingly beautiful room. It had a panoramic view that included a metropolitan area with towering structures, all connected by numerous bridges. Some of these edifices had unusual, artistically designed, shapes and forms. I particularly liked one building that appeared to be stacked in layers, leaning to one side. The variety of shapes and colors made these necessary edifices aesthetically pleasing. I supposed it also reduced the stress level that large metropolitan cities imposed, in this case, Nebadon beings.

From my window, I could see tiny vehicles, as well as little

Nebadons, flying back and forth over these bridges. They were not required to be inside bubbles as they were in their own environment. They looked like children from this distance and moved about at very high rates of speed, comically darting here and there. Above and all around the towering skyscrapers were small vessels flying in different directions. Each building had its own landing strip on top. I tried to look down, but couldn't see the ground. I didn't know if I was in an extremely high building or suspended in the air. I saw flashes of different colored lights that appeared to be connected to the traffic of flying beings and vessels. I had lost all sense of time and wasn't sure if it was night or day, although it appeared dark outside. Didn't they ever rest?

My bed was adorned with pillows of various sizes and shapes in colors varying from dark blue, lavender and lime green along with two other warm colors I could not identify. They were made out of a high quality silk-like material. They were beautiful. The bedspread had a soft glow the color of white linen. There were several sheer panels of material draped from the ceiling all around the bed, in colors that matched the pillows.

It was beginning to look irresistibly comfortable when Amie entered after a few polite knocks. "How do you like your room?" she asked.

"It's beautiful. How is yours?"

"I do not require one," she said.

I then remarked about the buildings outside and how high up we were. She said, "We are not connected to the planet. We are suspended above it."

"Why?"

"They discovered that by being suspended above the ground

they could avoid earthquakes, floods and other environmental events that were detrimental to their safety, by being suspended above the ground. More recently however, they have invented a way to control the weather and the climate is now consistently moderate over the entire planet. They have remained above the planet because the air is more pure there. The ground itself is only used for harvesting vegetation and water. There are areas where medicinal plants are cultivated and forests are maintained to stabilize the climate. The ground is considered sacred. They are able to preserve it and can erect more buildings and homes above the ground, never outgrowing the population's needs."

"Very wise," I said with a big yawn.

"Good night," Amie said and quickly exited my room. I chuckled to myself.

I was becoming used to her oddities. At least I was glad that she cleared up the fact that it was indeed night here.

I flopped face down into the soft comfort of the bed and began to drift off into a welcome sleep when I heard a soft knock at the door. I got up, still dressed, and opened it. There, floating in a bubble, was another Nebadon. This time it was a female. She was about two and a half feet tall with white hair draped softly over her shoulders. Her kind, wise eyes also bulged but were a beautiful emerald green. She didn't have as many deep wrinkles in her forehead and I guessed she was younger than the male I had encountered earlier, or perhaps she used some fabulous age-defying serum they had discovered.

"Do you need anything at all to make your stay more comfortable?" she asked, in a beautiful melodic voice. I didn't want to appear rude, but I was a bit hungry. Before I mentioned it, she told me just think of whatever I wanted to have for a meal and then touch the small door next to the bed. I thanked her and asked to know her name.

"I'Lera," she responded, then floated away.

I found the door, about two feet square, set into the wall. I touched it. A tray slid out with grilled fish, a variety of colorful vegetables, all of which I did not recognize, and a generous helping of something similar to couscous. The utensils were comical, like they had been shaped for toddlers, but I didn't mind. I sipped the tea and was happy it was the same ginger and floral herbal tea as before. It was a perfect meal.

After dinner, I lay back on the bed and fell asleep watching the delightful scene outside my window of little Nebabons busily darting every which way over their bridges, some flying around in tiny aircraft that landed and took off from the tops of their buildings. It was like a fairy tale. Their lights twinkled and soft colorful beams searched the sky for travelers needing to land. Right before I drifted off, I saw a huge mothership rise slowly into the sky beyond the city of buildings and bridges. It was like a monster raising its head from a secret hiding place. It continued to rise dwarfing the city. I imagined the many tiny people inside operating this huge spacecraft and the many small aircrafts that would fly off from it when it reached wherever it was headed. I couldn't believe what I was seeing. In one swift movement, it took off to the right, disappearing before my eyes.

I was weary from this 'wondrous land of Oz' and fell asleep envisioning Urantia in a similar advanced era of peace and harmony.

I woke up thinking about Amie. I had to come to terms with her. I couldn't put it off any longer. It was still dark outside and I had probably only slept three or four hours. I had been told that Amie was void of feelings and only had one purpose: my safety. I knew different. She did have feelings. Had they lied? Were the Nebadons capable of creating a physically superior beings? Of course they were. The androids were created to keep Zio and the Enlil safe. The confrontation between the fallen angels and the Enlil was the turning point in Urantia's future.

I didn't consider Amie to be an impersonal android, a machine. She was a person created by a superior race. So was I. The Nephallim had come to earth in ancient times instantly evolving us to a higher state and some even mating with us. We were a product of experimentation, Amie and I. I missed the uncomplicated life I had before I met Hank. It wasn't his fault; I had already been quantum leaping all my life and at least now I knew why. Life isn't like a dream, void of responsibility, drifting in and out of existence, soon forgotten. Each life is a span of time in a someone's consciousness and we either find purpose for existence realizing our connection to Our Creator or we drift off somewhere else and start over again and again until we get it right. It didn't matter how it ended or when. It was the stuff in between that was important - how we deal with it. We either figured it out or we mearly live, eat, sleep and die. I drifted off again, finally.

The next morning, I woke up to the wonderful scent of fresh coffee. Would the small door in the wall near the bed reveal breakfast? I touched it and out came coffee, a slice of whole-wheat bread grilled in what smelled like coconut oil, and a fried egg covered with cheese. A glass of the Ziot's green muck was also there. Okay, so I won't have withdrawal symptoms, I thought.

I had just finished eating when Amie rushed in after two

73

quick knocks on the door. "We have to get going. It's safe to return to Zio and the conditions will be just right if we leave now," she said.

I quickly changed clothes and followed her down a hallway toward a humming sound. "I was beginning to like it here though," I said. "So much for the vacation of a lifetime in the land of Oz." A door slid open, and just like the one that brought us here was a little vessel, just large enough for the two of us, hovering off the end of a ramp. Giving the urgency of the moment, I quickly entered it, secured my helmet, and buckled up. We were immediately whisked off towards Zio. I was put to sleep once again until we left the Nebadon atmosphere. When I woke up, the ride was again very bumpy passing through the energy vortex. To avoid seeing everything in multiplicities, I closed my eyes. Once we entered the wormhole, everything calmed down and it was smooth sailing, faster than I could ever comprehend, but nevertheless smooth.

While in flight, I turned to Amie and asked, "Why do you stay in the wall in my room?"

She slowly turned to me while processing my question and said, "You have to understand that there are many levels of existence and purpose. We are all different and yet all connected. It is not important for us to know why, it is only important to respect each other in our mutual quest to return to our Creator in the center of the universe, the *Hovana*."

She knew I knew. "Okay, I understand," I said.

She confided in me by adding, "We were told that if we showed our emotions and weaknesses, we would be returned and disassembled. It was predicted that humans would have great difficulty accepting androids like myself. You are the only one who figured it out. It might have been better if the

Nebadons had made us less complex, but they are kind hearted and very creative. I think they couldn't resist playing god."

"I consider you a friend, Amie. I want for your safety as much as you want for mine."

"You are my first assignment", she said, maybe my last. We are soon to join a great battle that will determine the future of Urantia."

Suddenly my head was flung against the side of the aircraft. It stunned me, but my helmet absorbed the hit. I had heard several quick shots on the side of our vessel, but nothing penetrated its walls. Amie was shouting, "We're hit! Source unknown! Request defensive mode immediately!"

Three enemy vessels swept into position and kept pace with us. The two were triangular shaped traveling on either side of us while the third larger ship, shaped like a squid kept steady formation in front of us. Amie shouted again, "Identification and source: Reptoid Urantia."

I felt a wave of terror start in my stomach and then consume my brain in an instant. Before I even had time to react, there was nothing, absolutely nothing anywhere. Was I dead? My stomach told me I was floating. I felt like I was on a roller coaster, only there was nothing to see, not even my body. So this is it? You just float around in nothing?

Then I heard, "Ninety degrees right." I recognized Amie's staccato, monotone speech. A Nebadon operator conversed with her. It was the first time I had heard their native tongue. He spoke in a melodic, soft language resembling French. The pilot maintained a steady, calm voice. I immediately saw the vessel to the right of us explode. Everything had returned now, my sight, my hearing. My head reeled as I tried to process what was happening.

Amie spoke to me now, "Sorry, I didn't have time to warn you. We were put in an invisible shield and had to travel upside down and sideways along the wall of the wormhole to keep from getting hit. The attackers were Reptoid from Urantia. All three attackers have been successfully annihilated."

I didn't respond. Amie locked her eyes on mine and evaluated me medically. "Advise for immediate shock treatment for subject upon arrival." I felt a cool liquid spray on my face and I fell asleep.

When I woke up, I was recovering in a small, metallic looking room. The familiar little disk-shaped machine was floating above me traveling over the length of my body back and forth making its ticking sound. When the attending Ziot was satisfied with the results, he took it and walked out with the disk under his arm. He had been the least friendly of all the Ziots I had encountered so far. Zero bed-side manner. Amie had been waiting outside. I joined her, and we walked back to our room. It felt good to return to my personal living quarters. Exhausted, I thanked Amie for all her expertise and her excellent performance on our trip and said good night. I watched her disappear into the wall as she had on many occasions, and again pondered the strangeness to which I had become accustomed. My best friend was now an android and my propensity for travel had exceeded my imagination, and , even that was a vast understatement. Tomorrow, I would enter the room labeled *The Awakening*. I longed for the simple life back in New Mexico, but there was no turning back now. I felt an allegiance to my fellow human beings, and sorrow for them. Minus certain governmental factions, the majority of people back home were unaware of the evil, destructive forces beneath Earth waiting to retake the planet in the final war of Armageddon. These people were at a great disadvantage. Those satanic aliens underground possessed supernatural powers genetically passed down to them. I wanted to take part in their destruction.

Suddenly, I heard a crackling sound like lightening and a blinding, white light filled the room. I had to cover my eyes. When the light dimmed, I slowly moved my hands away from my face. It was still bright, but I thought I could see a figure, a very tall, magnificent figure, on the other side of the room. It had bright blue eyes that continuously sparkled. I felt threatened by this overbearing presence. I called out to Amie. She ran out of the wall and stood in front of me with her laser gun raised and pointed it at the being, but then did nothing. I was stunned, but then I realized her quick analysis must have found this creature benign. Amie lowered her gun and the figure glided across the room towards me merely waving her aside like a fly. I tried to call for help, but couldn't speak. I pointed at the figure and attempted to push it away, but my body slammed into the wall behind me instead. With this act interpreted as aggression, Amie ran up to the being who reached out and touched her forehead with a finger stopping, her frozen in time, while still gazing straight ahead at me. "Please let her live!" I screamed. She dropped to the ground. He continued to approach me until he was standing uncomfortably close. I feared for my life but could not move. The being finally spoke. "You are quite the human specimen."

"Well, I've tried to take care of myself... eat right... exercise. You have a thing for women from Urantia? You know it's a pretty big universe out there."

"Silence!" He shouted in ten voices at once that continued to echo, making me shake violently. He seemed to have ignored my nervous chatter but then I had interrupted him as well, as he impolitely stood there savoring my natural scent. He finally backed away. Condescendingly, he said, "So, you're going to save your planet, are you?"

"I'm certainly going to try."

"You just may succeed. In answer to your question, yes, I find the women of Urantia enticing. But committed my crime of passion long ago. I've suffered my penance and experienced the most horrid death by being separated from The Source of Light and Love. He is a loving Creator though. I have been forgiven, but I live for eternity in shame."

"It was my followers who have not asked to be forgiven. They still think they are greater than Him. Satan is the worst abomination of all. I think it is very admirable that you want to try to overcome the offspring of the fallen angels. I truly do hope you succeed. This evil needs to come to an end, and the evolution of your people must resume on the path to a wondrous, elevated existence. I wish you the very best in your endeavors."

He started to fade and I whispered, "Who are you?"

The blinding light and the crackling, electric sound returned. I had to cover my eyes again. Suddenly I felt his warm breath on my neck and then he tasted me sliding his wet tongue slowly up the side of my face. Too scared to move or look, I heard him whisper in my ear, "Lucifer."

My knees buckled and trembeling all over I slid down the wall to the floor. Amie began to move, got to her feet slowly, checked the room visually. "He's gone," I said with mixed feelings.

# 9. THE AWAKENING

ALTHOUGH I WAS PRETTY SURE my latest acquaintance was quite motivated to avoid sin and stay in God's good graces, I still woke up frequently during the night. Checking shadows, listening for the crackling sound, and staying on edge kept me from getting a good night's sleep.

I rose early just as the first light crested over my white wall, bringing with it a painting of soft pastels. I took my time bathing and dressing for what probably would be the most eventful day of my life, and wondered what The Awakening would bring. I hoped it wouldn't be painful.

At breakfast, I couldn't help but notice the excitement in people's voices. A Swedish gentleman sitting across from me sensed my bewilderment. He told me that the seven billionth soul had been born on our home planet. This, I knew, signaled the beginning of Armageddon. I doubted my readiness for this event. Anxiety set in as I had an overwhelming desire to flee. A Ziot touched my shoulder with his long, thin hand. He said to be calm, and trust, in my instincts and him. His touch and voice calmed me immensely. I didn't have the ability to calm down that quickly on my own. Feeling no pain, as if I had just finished two margaritas, I followed him without a care in the world as he lead me out of the room and down the hall.

We entered a room that was tucked away at the end of the compound. The double doors were golden with the concentric circle symbol in the center, carved of silver. Above it were the words The Awakening. The room was dimly lit in blue. There were several other Ziots standing in a line at the front of the room. My guide took my hand and what happened next took me to another level of consciousness, both mentally and physically. The remaining Ziots encircled us; bowing their heads while illuminating themselves green. They reached out, and touched me from my shoulders to the top of my head. A strong, muscular, and decidedly female figure, with round breasts and nipples that showed through a filmy and loosely-draped gown slowly began to descend from above. This being sent rays of purple and red through me. I felt a burning sensation deep in the pit of my stomach that slowly circulated outward through my entire body. My upper back began to hurt with an intense pain. I heard myself scream out in an unknown voice from deep inside me. I bowed my head and the internal voice repeated the following words twice,

*"I exalt Thee, I honor Thee, I kneel before Thee."*
I dropped to the floor on my knees. Exhausted, I retreated

into myself protecting myself, like a wounded animal and covering my body with my.... wings!

The pain ceased. Relieved, I stood erect. I felt so strong! As I glanced around, I was confused at first. All of the objects around me, including the walls, looked transparent. I quickly adjusted to this, but then flinched, covering my ears, at the sound of someone walking in the hallway. Sound, light, all sensory input, seemed magnified. My skin now possessed a luminous, translucent quality and had metallic, silvery glow. I was taller. I must have grown by about two feet. I enjoyed the transformation, but found it initially difficult to adjust to my larger size. I was cramped in this same room now, my head almost brushed the ceiling. This soon passed as well, and I found my larger size and hightened senses had given me a tremendous feeling of peace and confidence. I was a being miraculously awakened and transformed,and yet myself, a human being from Urantia.

The Ziots began their deep throat singing, which I had learned to love and found comforting. The spiritual being above me, which I now recognized as The Ziots' leader referred to biblically as the Archangel Gabriel, recited the following verse:

*"Infinite Mind inspires you.*
*Infinite Power expresses through you.*
*Infinite Life heals you,*
*And presents you as a true spiritual being.*
*You have put on the new man,*
*Which is renewed in knowledge,*
*In the image of Him that created you."*

The Ziots bowed to her and then she vanished. My guiding

Ziot took my hand again. I was instantly flying through space, seeing everything from a different perspective. The other Ziots were also there, some to my sides and some behind in ceremonial procession. The experience was phenomenal. I had never imagined it could be like this.

As we passed each star, I was able to see it in it's entirety, all the way through to the other side. I had pellucid visions, seeing in all dimensions at once. If I wanted to understand what I viewed beyond multidimensional, I could separate parts showing me how an object fit together and I instantaneously comprehended all particles in mathematical equations.

A meteorite startled me as it rushed toward us, and my guide said, "Push it away." I pointed to it and it immediately began moving in the opposite direction. Another one was hurling through space even faster toward us, and he said, "Dissolve it."

"What? But, how?"

It was about to slam into me. "Help me! I don't know!" Suddenly, the thought of just picturing it dissolved came to me. As I stared at it, it turned to grey clay and crumble, disintegrated.

"I can dissolve the enemy this way? I can just make things just go away, make them cease to exist?"

"You are supernatural," he said. "You can do anything you can imagine."

"I can even lose ten pounds in a split second?" He didn't respond, but turned and looked at me with a compassionate expression and a half smile. He still liked humor.

Back in the learning room labeled The Awakening, my guide informed me that I was the last Urantian to come to Zio. He explained the battle would begin as soon as the Greys, Reptillians, and the Nordic races of aliens living beneath my planet began to show themselves.

"The Reptillians, a variety of Draconians, and their workers, the Greys, have been trying to control your planet for years with considerable success. They know of Zio, they know who is here, and what has been taking place here. You can expect them to try to intercept your return to Urantia. They can shape shift into human form, just as you are able to transform. This is possible because they, and you, are interdimensional beings."

He was levitating, slowly floating up and down, while telepathically communicating with me. I had never eperienced anything like this before, my time with Zio, the way they transported themselves, changed to fluorescent color and communicated without the use of speech. I should have predicted his next move. He stopped moving, remained motionless, and continued, "You will be able to see into the fourth dimension, even in your human form and use this guise to recognize the true nature of all you encounter, because you are receptive to the vibrations from which all things are created.

I sat down, confounded with all this information about my new abilities. It was hard to believe I was so changed now, so different.

Sensing this, he sat beside me and took my hand in his. "Do not allow negativity in any form to enter your body. Thoughts are real. They can drain your power. Relax and trust yourself and trust the One who gave your ancestors, and many others in other worlds, the same abilities.

I took a deep breath and he continued. "To you, these vibrations will seem as natural as hearing a sound. Creatures living beneath the earth all project a illusions that most humans are only capable of visually interpreting as another human. They also have supernatural powers, as they are the descendants of the fallen angels.

"Remember, there are many who have transmorqified into people in key government positions. Occasionally, you will see alien creatures in an incomplete transformation.Their pupils will appear as a thin vertical line, the eyes of a reptile, instead of round like yours. You must, above all, trust your instincts. They will never fail you. Your android, Amie, has been created and designed to aid you and will return to Urantia with you. She will be necessary to protect you while you are in your human form, but you will surpass her abilities when transformed. She will then be dependent on you, and will follow your instructions. When using your wings to transport yourself, remember that your speed may take you through other dimensions of space and time. You will have to get used to this. Amie has been programmed to time travel with considerable ease. One last thing; the only way you can take her with you when you are flying is for her to ride on your back. It will be up to you to take her or leave her as deemed necessary at the time."

"How will I know what to do?" I asked. "I've never fought in war before."

"There are key figures like yourself already in position on Urantia who bear the symbol of the trinity, the all knowing eye. You will recognize them in the fourth dimension, the dimension veiled to the average human. They are the Nordics, and are descendants of the Annunaki who did not follow Satan in the early years of Urantia. They are Watchers like yourself who have remained hidden under Mount Shasta in California and under the arctic region. They have been observing your planet as it draws closer to the evolution of your race.

"Nordics are tall, blond and all have blue eyes. They are the High Enlils who will lead you. They despise the Enki; They will be your family.

"You must keep your identity hidden until the real battle takes place. You are a human being with awakened, supernatural powers. These powers are sacred, bestowed by our Creator. They originated with your ancestors at the beginning of time on your planet. Trust your instincts and gain the planet back for its rightful residents. You will be able to transform physically at will, but you must be transformed in order to use your powers. You are still vulnerable while in your human form. Do you have any concerns?"

"Will I remain there afterwards? Will I ever die?" I asked.

"You must remain, because you are a descendant of the Watchers. This has been your destiny and purpose from birth assigned by the One True Spirit, the Alpha and the Omega. You have been awakened and that will be your fate, to continue to protect your planet. No, you will never die."

He paused and then said, "Our mission is complete here."

"Thank you," I said as they all ascended at once. I knew I would never see them again.

JOANNE JOHNSON

# 10. THE DETAILS

DURING DINNER, A TALL ANDROID with the title *Mission Specialist* introduced himself in order to explain the method of travel that would return all six-hundred of us back to Urantia. Aside from his fluorescent orange hair, whimsically chosen by his Nebadon creators, he had an appearance usually associated with a high-ranking military personnel that demanded respect. He apologized for using complicated terminology and said he would simplify his lecture as much as possible, but at the same time did not want to insult our intelligence.

"The method of travel we'll be using to return to Urantia was developed through a collaboration between the Nebadons and the Iconians. The Iconians are our allies, and were forced to abandon their planet one hundred years ago. The Iconian

Gateway is still the most effective passage for in universal travel known to us at this time. A binding contract was signed, allowing the Iconians to return to their planet as long as they remained peaceful. In return they offer us the use of their gateway.

"The way the gateway works is by creating a quantum tunnel from a fixed position on Zio, a planet in this case, through a wormhole that allows for space travel using zero space time. There is a built-in operational mechanism to stabilize our own quantum state wave function as we pass through the tunnel. The craft will approach the boundary, disappear momentarily, and reappear on the other side of it. Safe transportation within normal time scales has been perfected by the Nebadons and used by them for eighty years now. Some of your scientists have come somewhat close to this concept using quantum physics, but there is still much room for expansion in their theories. It is my opinion that they obsess too much over the speed of light and Einstein's theory of relativity. Light has no speed," he chuckled.

He continued by saying, "Anyway, reguarding to your spacecraft. It is the most mechanically superior craft created by the Nebadons have created. As we will later see, it resembles the natural shape of a fish, and is capable of handling any situation. With this form of travel, there is one thing in particular to consider: we will not be able to determine the exact landing location on Urantia, only the most likely spot. Your ship is equipped to land anywhere—even an ocean, desert, or mountaintop. There will be no need for adaptive devices while inside the spacecraft and it will feel as if we have arrived in seconds. There will be no loss of time whatsoever."

This caused murmurs among people in the dining room. It

these were miraculous achievements by our human standards.

He continued on, "The Draconians, Reptillians and Greys are only equipped to interrupt a tunnel from a sideways entry if they receive an alert to our presence. However, they have not completely perfected their entry. Although they continue to work on this, they do occasionally suffer consequences, which are, of course, deadly in the worst way. Can you imagine yourself molecularly broken apart with all your pieces left to float in space? Not to worry. This will not happen to you."

"Draconians, Reptillians and Greys are extremists. The loss of life to reach a goal is incidental and unimportant to them. Remember, they thrive in atmospheres of hatred and fear. If you have no other weapon, remaining in a state of calmness, void of emotions will buy you time. It confuses them."

"Now, if you will form a line to my right when you are finished with dinner, you will receive your microscopic chip. It will be painlessly inserted into your right arm just above the wrist. This year, a one-world currency was established on Urantia, as some of you may already know. You have all been supplied with an adequate number of credits in your "bank account" as it was once referred to as on your planet. Use the currency to take care of all your necessities while in your human form. Also a vaccination swab will be passed over your tongues to protect you against all viruses and diseases on Urantia, as well as a few possible unusual ones, as the underground aliens try their hand at biological warfare before revealing themselves. Thank you, and good luck."

He exited the dining room with an air of urgency in his gait.

I barely slept that night. I could not imagine myself taking part in the most important battle our planet would ever see that could either result in the instantaneous evolution of mankind, or dominance by an army of satanic aliens forcing mankind into a wretched existence for eternity. I longed, again, for the simplicity of my former life, as I took one last look around my personal space. I was already missing its serene atmosphere.

I had learned many lessons on Zio and had no regrets. I was finished with trying to figure out why this was all happening to me and I accepted my inevitable destiny as a result of my ancestry. It certainly explained my lack of attachment to others and why I had always found it unnecessary to have close, binding relationships. Somehow, I had been aware of the ticking clock inside me, drawing me closer to my real destiny. Quantum leaping while asleep, for most of my life, and the resulting exotic space travel made everything else seem boring and meaningless. But now, the feeling of unfinished business had left me. In its place, I felt direction and purpose.

Morning came, and Amie and I prepared to enter the spacecraft assigned to us. It really does resemble a fish. I thought. Its head was connected to its body by a smaller segment. I suspected the head was where the android pilots were located. Passengers were being escorted to enter the body of the fish. I noticed a fancy-looking apparatus located at the very back, that tucked under itself and bear the symbol of the all-knowing eye, The Trinity.

We were handed small black boxes as we entered, and we're required to receive a tiny prick in the back of our heads, administered by an android using a small gold cylinder that emitted colorful beams of light. After Amie and I were seated, I looked at the box I had been given. Inside were two shiny silver bullets, each about five inches long. Attached about midway on each bullet was a small ring. I noticed they both fit my ring fingers perfectly.

A pleasant, female voice began to speak. I saw her hologram at the head of the aisle. She told us we were already programmed to be dropped off in very remote locations and would have to make our own way to civilization. She further explained that if our landing was off course, we would need to be prepared for anything. In the event we land in a more popoulated area were, our sudden appearance would only last a half second as if we stepped out of thin air. The only instructions we had were to keep a low profile; find accommodations, food, and any other necessities; then wait. One Nordic was already assigned to each of us and would make contact shortly after our arrival. A picture of a typical male Nordic was displayed for us. A tall, lean humanoid with long white-blonde hair he had very strong facial features, such as a wide square jaw and deep-set piercing blue eyes.Then a female Nordic was displayed. She was still also tall and thin, with long blond hair and blue eyes. She would have made a fortune as a high-fashion model. They were both beautiful.

We were then briefed on the microscopic chip implantation. It had an integrated circuit for security purposes, that had been inserted into the back of our heads. It was described as our communication system and universal information source, a "mental visual notebook" to be used visually, aurally, and telepathacally. It could call it up at will, and Information would be given to us mentally, to allow for our freedom of movement. , if necessary, a hologram would appear in front of us to provide a visual aide. The system was completely telepathic and thought sensitive. If someone attempted to contact us, a very soft beeping sound would be heard in our right ear. A conversation could then take place. All contact signals were untraceable. Our first instructional hologram then disappeared.

There was one other, rather strange item. In the pocket of our seats it was a small envelope with a note attached, explaining that the envelope contained special instructions, and would self-destruct ten seconds after being opened. I wondered how long the instructions were, and if there were any slow readers on board. I opened mine. It read: "Reptilians and Greys are violently allergic to sugar. They will suffocate immediately upon contact with it. Always carry candy. Never leave home without it." The note, then disintegrated in my hand.

"Is this a joke?" I wondered. I looked in my seat pocket and located several wrapped hard candies. I glanced around and saw others stuffing their pockets with the candies. Some were laughing out loud. Then I remembered that Ziots appreciated good humor. They had had the last laugh on us. Good for them!

Another hologram appeared, this time a male android. He began an explanation of the silver bullets. "Your weapon is extremely dangerous and lethal. They are designed to create an exact microscopic version of a black hole in outer space. They will automatically be activated upon your departure of our spacecraft. Once you shoot your victim, it will completely dissolve them. You carry a bullet concealed inside your hand secured by inserting your finger through its ring. They should fit you and your android perfectly. You fire it with your thumb by aiming it at your target then pushing the button located on the left side of it. The button is reversed for those of you who are left-handed. It shoots a tiny, black ball that silently hits its target and spreads, freezing every molecular part of their body. It is a very painful death. For a quick death, we suggest aiming at the brain. The loss of a limb, for example, would result in a slower death as flesh, tissue, and veins turn to ice crystals and disappear. It will move on to organs and finally to bones until there is no trace of your target. Your victim will be preoccupied if hit; and will discontinue attack. There is no limit to the self-creating black holes of your silent weapon. All the passengers applauded loudly. As I joined in, I thought The Nebadons had truly outdone themselves.

"We are about to depart, so if you wish, you can call up your mental notebook and command it to show you our fleet in transit. However, you may be disappointed, as it will only last a few seconds. Our command spacecraft will be in the lead, with the other two following. If your seats have the Roman numeral I on them, you are in the commander's spacecraft. II and III will follow in that order. Enjoy your trip and good luck."

I decided not to watch, but instead to listen to music, and try to relax. The seat in front of me had the Roman number I. I wasn't sure I wanted to see the wormhole as we entered it. I was VERY nervous. I looked over at Amie and she seemed fine. She inspected her silver bullet, and then placed it back in their box and stored them in her backpack. She then turned and smiled at me. That helped.

I distracted myself by thinking that we'd have to change the color of her hair once we arrived. It might pass in some punk groups, but its fluorescent green hair would surely draw attention to us, almost anywhere we landed.

"Amie," I asked, "What would you think about being a brunette like me?"

She looked at me blankly as if making a choice about her appearance was never offered to her before.

She finally responded, "Okay."

"We'll have to buy you some normal clothes, too. I guess you'll have to literally come out of the closet," I laughed. "No more wall to hide in. How would that feel?"

"I don't know. I'm not sure how it will feel."

I knew Amie would have no problem adjusting to oEarth's environment. She had extremely fine-tuned adapting skills. I hoped we could enjoy ourselves a short while before the battle began. With a never-ending credit supply and her ability to speak any language, we could enjoy a grand vacation.

I stopped this thought abruptly as I reminded myself of our mission and its importance. I never in my wildest dreams could have imagined any of this. 'What a great sci-fi novel all this would make.' I thought. A quick jerk sent my head back into the seat. Are we already there?

# 11. GOING HOME

I felt another sudden jolt that knocked me almost completely out of my seat. Some of the passengers were looking around with concerned expressions. A pilot began speaking, "We have encountered alien intrusion. As this was expected, it will only delay us a few minutes, and then we can resume our direction. Please pull down the padded bar located on the back of the seat in front of you until it locks in position in front of your body. It will help brace you. We have this completely under control. You may watch if you wish by calling up your mental notebook telepathically. Sorry for the inconvenience."

I needed to know what was going on, so I immediately called up my screen. I had a cockpit view now. I looked over at Amie and saw she was also observing it. Something was coming closer and I closed my eyes, worried it would crash into us. When I opened my eyes again there was nothing but space in front of us. There was another spacecraft at ninety degrees to our side. It dropped below us and out of sight. Amie, open the window shade! I shouted. There it was in all its ugly, Reptilian glory – a ship with scales, red snake eyes, and a cockpit resembling a lizard head. It's pilot was looking straight at me. I wanted to scream, but quickly covered my mouth choking down the terror I felt as our eyes locked.

What I saw next I'll never forget, and maybe it was good that it happened, because I then knew what to expect from our advanced weaponry. Suddenly, the nose of the lizard's spacecraft seemed to fall to pieces, then the cockpit bit by bit. Everything separated into tiny parts. I saw the pilot's face with his mouth open. He was screaming as he crumbled away, until his face was no more. The rest of the spaceship followed suit, the last remaining parts separating and falling into space. My God, what a horrible death, I thought. It must have started at his feet and worked upwards. Welcome to the flip side of technology.

I contemplated about the Nebadons with all their scientific achievements: and wondered where spiritual and moral consciousness drew the line. Then I remembered what a Ziot had said to me in training. "They have found a balance between their Creator and scientific advancement." The Nebadons were in an era of magical rather than technological achievement. It alluded to a higher consciousness and a more advanced spiritual lifestyle. My own personal, moral justification in an expansion of the commandment, thou shall not kill. It went something like this; 'Protect all life against evil, destructive aggressors.' It worked for me.

I searched the hologram screen for more invaders from the cockpit view and found none. There was just the back of our pilot's head and beyond that dark, peaceful space. Amie was pulling the shade down and I wondered how much time had gone by.

A relaxing, silent five minutes passed. I thought I heard a faint beeping sound in my right ear, but wasn't sure. Was someone calling me?

"Hello?"

"Well, hello. I see your ship is on its way back to Urantia. Had a preview of those nasty, Reptilian bastards, I see."

"Hank? Is that you?"

"Yep. You're due to land at 9:30 p.m. New Mexico time."

"Hank! So much has happened. It seems like such a long time ago since we met."

"Time is irrelevant and rather warped here on Urantia in my opinion," he said. "I'm contacting you to remind you that if you get in any tight spots or need help you can call on me. I will do my best to make this assignment go smooth for you."

"Thank you, Hank. It sure will be good to see you again."

"What – my old, bony, hairy self? See you later."

An announcement from the pilot began, " We have successfully exited the Gateway and are close to entering your solar system. We will be passing through a giant bubble of gas caused by the supernovae of a cluster of stars about ten million years ago. This will not disturb our spacecraft. However the bubble is highly magnetized and will eventually cause a pole shift on your planet as your solar system passes through. This will result in a cataclysmic purification of the planet consummated by earthquakes, floods, extinction of species and upheavals of human societies. As you know, this process has already begun, and it will be finalized with the beginning of a new sun or solar age. All Urantians and the physical planet itself will be awakened to new potentialities, to new and higher energies. The alien races, the Enki living beneath your planet, will show themselves before this. They do not want your species to evolve. They want the planet for themselves and plan to take it over before it becomes more difficult.

"You will leave this ship, with your androids, in groups of ten. Scatter - do not stay together. You are too valuable. Your intended drop-off location will be shown to you as you exit. We will be arriving at the first location in ten seconds. Prepare to disembark and good luck."

Ten seconds felt like twenty minutes. My seat was numbered seven. The moment I had been anticipating was suddenly here. I was going home and I didn't care where they put me. The hologram screen showed a map of Europe with Amsterdam, Holland was accentuated. A highly pressurized, hydraulic sound announcede a hatch in the spacecraft. Many hands reached out to us in loving support as the first ten awakened Enlils walked down the aisle to the opening. The oriental woman, Ting, stopped me as I passed her to give me a hug and whispered, "Until we meet again, may God be with you."

"And with you also, Ting," I responded as I waved goodbye.

As we approached the opening, a force gently lifted us into the air and then lowered us until our feet touched the ground. Amie and I walked to the top of a grassy hill. I watched the spacecraft whiz away and lamented having to leave the bizarre, yet wonderful life I had come to know on Zio. When I turned around, the others were already out of sight.

While Amie and I walked, I conveniently pulled up audio information from my microchip. I listened to the weather, learning that Holland was generally rainy, with October being the wettest month. It was October 6th. I quickly checked our location, finding us approximately five miles from Amsterdam. Not bad. I hoped the others would have this much luck with their assigned drop locations.

Night was falling here, and I caught a glimpse of a distant windmill silhouetted by moonlight through the parting clouds. It seemed to greet us with its old world charm. The terrain was distinctly rural. Through the misty rain and down a small, winding road, a streetlight revealed an old stone farmhouse with wooden shutters. Through sheer-white lace curtains, I saw a fire still glowing in the fireplace. I enjoyed this brief glimpse into the life of whoever lived inside, allowing it to soothe my soul, longing for easier times and my old home. The mantel was adorned with delicate little blue and white delft treasures, a sign of considerable affluence. The scent of a hearty stew still lingered near as we passed by.

It was now I fully realized my responsibility to my fellow man. It was my job to protect people like this and assure the continuation of the intended plan of evolution. We have suffered enough, I thought. Death, sickness, war, and environmental disasters were just a few of the perils we had undergone. Finally, all these would be eliminated forever, allowing humans their rightful endowments and a glorious life of abundance. I rejoiced in knowing that moment was near at hand. However, we would likely undergo far worse than we have thus far before we achieve our final bliss.

The clouds parted again, this time exposing a barn perched on top of the next hill. It was almost hidden behind a grove of large trees, seasonably leafless, with aging, yet gracefully twisting trunks. We entered through the barn's heavy, creaking old door and took refuge in its modest comfort. I located the metallic thermal blanket in my backpack and indulged myself in its warmth. The temperature outside was falling rapidly. Exhausted from the excitement of our arrival, I welcomed a soft bed of straw; but first I called up the correct time from my integrated circuit chip. About two and a half feet in front of me, red numbers conveniently displayed themselves. It was 12:30 a.m., five and a half hours until the first break of dawn.

"Amie, will you wake us at 5:30?" I asked.

A cow voiced her objection to our presence and then was silent. Amie seemed fascinated by this black and white spotted creature. She slowly turned away from the cow and said, "Yes, of course."

A rooster startled me from sleep and I jumped to my feet. "Is it already morning?" I asked Amie.

"It is 5:00 am," she said as she gathered our backpacks up off the ground. It was still dark outside.

Suddenly the large, barn door flew open. Standing in the doorway was a very tall, white-bearded man in denim overalls, wooden shoes, and a furry aviators hat that covered his ears. My heart was pounding as I said, "Geode morgen! he said. I quickley replied prettige dag and then realized too late I'd mistakenly said 'have a nice day.'

# 12. URE

THE MAN LET OUT A BIG, HEARTY LAUGH and raised his right hand in a universal peace greeting. I understood him telepathically to say, "Good day. I am Nordic." I felt immensely relieved. When I got a closer look at him, I saw he was lean and muscular with white-blond hair and deep blue eyes. His long beard gave him an older demeanor. Although he was only about forty years old. He could have easily passed for a Dutch or Scandinavian farmer.

"Quickly, we must go. Does she have nothing else to wear?" He asked. "We must do something about the green hair. It brings attention to us."

I quickly fumbled through my backpack and handed Amie some clothes, and then a hat, instructing her to stuff all her hair inside it. She stripped where she stood and changed in front of us. I hadn't cinsidered that she wouldn't be accustomed to the same feelings about modesty humans were. I wondered if she had slept or just gone into idle, lying in the straw next to me? Did she like lying down instead of just standing all night? I hoped the opportunity to learn more about her would present itself now that we were here.

"You must maintain a very low profile until you fine tune your skills of hybrid and alien recognition. If you do recognize one, do not react. Stay calm and they will not recognize you. If you experience fear, they will sense it and spot you. Understand?"

"Yes. What should I call you?"

"I am Ure. You have a given Enlil name. Do you wish to know it?"

"Yes, of course. I wasn't aware I had one."

"Anna Ray," he said. A dream from the past suddenly raced across my mind of a woman wearing a dark, blue gown with long, black hair. She had been riding bareback on a horse and came bearing the message, "Anna Ray". It had puzzled me and then was forgotten, until now. My parents had named me Anne. I wondered if Ray had been added as an implication of one of my dormant powers.

We took off on foot, down winding, country roads with the first light of day at our backs. An occasional windmill, small canal, a few cows and one old man carrying a bag over his shoulder were our only encounters. The little stucco and brick houses were getting closer together now and the traffic on the road had picked up. Soon we were walking through a village of cobblestone streets, and quaint little shops. The windows of all the houses were adorned with shutters and white lace curtains that were shorter than normal to make room for small plants on the windowsills. There was an occasional garden between the houses. It appeared to be the responseability of the elderly men in the village to tend to them. They wore thick wooden shoes to avoid the mud. Most had pipes hanging out of their mouths as they worked. The sound of women beating rugs and  mattresses and sweeping the walkways in front of their homes led me to imagine that cleanliness was a devotion here. Occasionally, someone would stop their chores to greet us with a smile and a nod.

We passed a vendor selling french fries and pickled herring in sour cream from a humble but adequate food cart. He kept the small jars of herring chilled on ice. The smell of  fried potatoes filled the air as he cooked them. This wonderful aroma made my stomach growl fiercely. I was famished. "Ure, do we have time to eat something?"

"Yes, but you must eat as we travel," he replied.

The vendor handed me a single jar of fish and then the fries in a brown, funnel-shaped paper cone. He tried to give me mayonnaise for the fries. I passed. A device that resembled an older style cell phone was passed over my wrist and the vendor nodded and said, "Danke." We immediately resumed our pilgrimage.

Bike, scooter, and foot traffic picked up.  As we crossed an old bridge Ure said, "We are entering Amsterdam now."

"Where are you taking us, Ure?" I asked while devouring the herring and fries.

"The basement of an old building, then underground where we will travel by tunnel to our home base."

Someone brushed up against me knocking my fries to the ground. I looked down at them with longing. I spun around to catch a better look and saw a man in a baseball hat walking away. He must have felt me staring because at him he stopped and turned very slowly. There it was! His face and body changed in a brief flash as I saw through the guise. He was a hybrid - half man and half reptilian. A very ugly sight! I could feel him carefully studying me with his Reptilian eyes, the eyes of a deadly snake about to strike its victim.

I heard, "Calm yourself and turn away." It was Ure. He knew I had recognized the Enki.

I quickly shifted gears and used my best strategy for calming. Conjuring up a memory of diving into a deep, blue pool on one of my past vacations, I imagined the coolness of the water on to my skin. I remembered how it felt to come to the surface for air. I concentrated on the details of this pool, listening to the sound of rushing water from a nearby waterfall. I focused on the feeling of the water's soft spray on my face, and felt myself relax.

The Reptilian turned away and walked in the opposite direction.

We traveled down a street with a canal on one side. I recognized the smell of marijuana in the air as we passed a houseboat that had abundant display of plants on its deck. Smoke rose from its cabin. At the end of this street, we turned down an alley and entered through an old weather-beaten red door under a fire escape. Just inside this door was a set of solid, metallic double doors bearing the engraved symbol of The Watchers, the all-knowing eye. There was no clear way to open them. Ure waved his hand in the air and the doors parted. Laser beams darted in all directions. I was aprehensive, but Amie ran analysis, and then I followed her in.

We were ushered into an enclosed bullet-shaped capsule that sat on an old train track. After buckling up, we were swept away at an unbelievable and terrifying speed. I was afraid my skin would stretch too far backwards and my face would never snap back again. Amie was wide-eyed in amazement, staring at me. This only increased my concern. Of course, her skin was artificial and didn't stretch.

I wondered where Ure was. With great difficulty, I managed to turn my head by making, jerking motions and looked behind us. A bright light seemed to be following us. I supposed he was in his own familiar mode of transportation, and I struggled to turn my head back around. The transport vessel then slowed and lowered itself to the ground.We arrived at another pair of metal doors that parted.

With much relief, I stepped out and felt my face, assuring myself it was still intact. I was immediately distracted by a magnificent sight. A space area three stories high, the size of a football stadium, was filled with huge screens attended by male and female Nordics who monitored our planet and outer space. They were all clothed in a silky, shimmering cloth that had iridescent glow. Maybe it was their skin; I wasn't sure yet. They were tall, fair, beautiful beings. My heart skipped when they all turned and greeted us, clasping their extended hands in front of them. I needed no translation for this offer of friendship. I felt a part of something important and wonderful and I returned the greeting. I was home and this was now my family.

JOANNE JOHNSON

# 13. DOING AMSTERDAM

We were shown a room with all the same conveniences found on Zio. The familiarity was comforting and probably intended.

"I suggest that you sleep here at night, but you and your android are free to roam the city during the day, of course. While in your human form, you are vulnerable, but once transformed, you will not require much sleep or protection. We share some of the same genes you and I. Your transformed height, for example, was carried down from your ancient ancestry making you the same height as Nordics. Also, all of your supernatural powers still intact. However, you will discover you have been gifted with two very powerful skills. Your given Enlil name, Anna Ray, was given to you due to a ray from your eyes that paralyze your target solidifies it and turns it to dust. You can also thrust your enemy or an object away from you in any direction by pointing them and then slice the target into smaller pieces by moving your finger in any direction. The rays are razor sharp, and most effective when your emotion is anger caused by evil. The destiny of the enemy is in your hands and their eventual doom your choosing. Nordics no longer require wings. Eventually you too will lose your wings, perhaps in about five hundred years."

"Oh, well, that's right around the corner. I look forward to it," I said, covering up my inability to comprehend my new life span.

I found satire to be a waste of time on Nordics, unlike the Ziots. I wondered if I would also lose my jovial zestfulness. It had always been my saving grace when I was a human.

Ure continued, "There has been an increase in activity at all of the entry ways to alien underground bases these past two days Urantia time. Also many alien spacecraft patrol outer space now. Posed as allies, promising a future of bliss that is disease free, and abundant in food and water. They'll concoct all sorts of magical illusions and lies to dazzle the human race. The anti-Christ will then emerge. Be ready. After that, there will be mass hysteria as the aliens attempt to take over the planet, destroying all who try to oppose them. Many Urantians will perish. Do not waste your power on just one Enki. We will disable their bases, and strike where they are weakest, using strategies we've developed over many years. These strategies will confuse them. We will overcome them as a group. You will find your supernatural powers more than adequate. You have not yet realized these in full. I have been appointed to assist you if needed. Welcome, and it has been my pleasure to meet you, Anna Ray."

I thanked Ure for his hospitality. He smiled at us as he walked away. Amie had been studying her screen. I tapped her shoulder wanting to get a good night's sleep. I was already dreading the ride back through the tunnel the next day. Surely there must be a more pleasant way to the surface.

Several Nordics had passed us and all had nodded, some had transformed into balls of light and then floated up to the higher levels of the base. Two, obviously male Nordics, had protruding bellies as if pregnant. "Amie, I asked, did you see the two males today? Were they pregnant?"

"My files describe Nordic males as capable of being impregnated as well as the females.The gestation period is five months."

"Oh. But how?"

"Through insemination or traditional mating," she responded. I wasn't sure how two males could mate traditionally as humans do, but decided to drop the subject. It wasn't really important in view of our present agenda.

Amie continued, "All Nordics make excellent, loving parents and partners because there is no traditional role-playing involved. There is only equality and respect between Nordic males and females."

I pondered this unusual concept for several minutes but kept yawning. Bedtime had never been so appealing. I kept talking to Amie about the Nordics, but she wasn't listening to me ramble. She was concentrating on her bed, feeling it, lying on it, then standing up again and staring at it. Fascinated, I continued to watch her as she tried to lie down in her bed. I was already under the covers. She looked over at me for a comparison check several times. It was amusing. I also had concern over what kind of life remained for her here after our mission was complete. Would we stay together? Would she want to marry and live like a human? If she married, she would not age, while her partner would. Nebadons had secretly given her human emotions. Why? I was uncomfortable having someone's whole existence dedicated to me alone. Perhaps the time would present itself for a heart to heart talk with her. Besides being female, we had another thing in common - we were both eternally indestructible. I fell asleep trying to imagine living forever; my most current fascination.

The next morning, we dressed hastily and set out tocheck out our new surroundings. Also we needed to change the color of Amie's hair and aquire new clothing. We found Ure busily monitoring a screen on the second level. He had been working all night. He didn't appear tired in fact he looked exactly the same as the night before. I asked if we could reach the streets another way to avoid the tunnel.

He told me that I could transform, and with Amie riding on my back we could use one of the air tunnels that went straight up to the street level. He said we should practice this, being very careful to quickly revert back to my human form before you appear in public. "If anyone sees you do this, pass your hand over their eyes and they will forget it. I meant to tell you that last night. If an alien or hybrid sees you do this, you must dispose of him immediately. You might as well begin to 'try your wings' as they say on Urantia."

I smiled as we walked away. Try your wings. The saying was actually kind of cute.

We found the air tunnel. At first, we stood there with blank expressions on our faces looking rather stupid. Finally, I said, "Here's the plan. Once I transform, I will lower myself so you can jump on my back. Then we will head straight up for the street. Hold on tight. It might be a bumpy ride at first until I get used to this."

"I have been equipped with excellent balance and gymnastic skills, so don't worry about me," she said.

After transforming, I had to take a moment to adjust to my new height. The ground appeared much farther away now. I held my wings close to my side, Amie jumped on, and I felt like a great bird with her on my back. We soared upward with amazing speed through the air tunnel. I flew up above the ground and then lowered myself back down with my wings spread out fully. I had overshot my destination. Amie slid off easily.

We were on an old cobblestone alley between two buildings. There, lying on the ground, was an emaciated, elderly man drinking wine from a bottle. I didn't mean to alarm him, but when I straightened up to my full height and lowered my wings, he dropped his bottle and hastened away crawling on all fours. I couldn't have that, so I reached down and passed one hand over his eyes. He fell asleep and I transformed back. I was able to read the microscopic chip in his wrist and saw he had no credits left. I abundantly replenished them. It was the least I could do for scaring him like that. We then walked towards the street.

The population above ground was busily going about their day. Jingling bells from a chanting Hare Krishna cult wearing their traditional orange robes, stole our attention. They were on the street corner and Amie wanted to watch them.

I had never seen so many bicycles in one place. A man with a flushed face and long blonde hair came out of nowhere, wearing a strange purple cape with a bright blue satin lining. He seemed to almost float across the square, his cape gently waved to a rhythm all its own. He had a following, a group that appeared to be his harem. They trailed behind him, in a sort of daze, and were all draped in a variety of bright sheer materials. I assumed they were all on drugs.

We found our way through the crowd to the front door of a salon. Upon entering, everyone turned to stare at us. Were we wearing 'Transformer and android from planet Zio' signs on our chests? I thought we looked fairly normal, but in Amsterdam, that made you look like a foreigner. Shopping for some very hip clothes, so as to blend in with one of the leading fashion-minded cities of the world, was now a matter of survival. I looked forward to it.

After asking to the beautician to change Amie's hair color to brunette, I lost myself in the mindless, but therapeutic world of a fashion magazine.

About forty-five minutes later, I was startled by a scream. I dropped the magazine to the floor when I saw Amie standing in the salon chair, her hair now brunette, warding off beauticians with what appeared to be various karate moves.

"Amie!" I screamed, "Get down!" She jumped out of the chair turned about three somersaults in the air, and landed on her feet on the floor.

"She's with the circus," I explained. "Sorry for the disturbance." I quickly grabbed her hand, paid the clerk with a wave of my wrist, and out the door we went. We walked for two blocks until I was sure we were far enough, then stopped. "Please explain what just happened in there," I demanded.

"They wanted to give me a Sassoon cut on one side and afix a purple feather in it, then shave my head on the other side, and buzz their salon logo into it as advertisement," she excitedly explained. "They said my head was perfectly shaped and this new style would be very attractive on me. Then they showed me a picture of how it would look. I don't want to advertise the fact that I'm a freak!"

"I should have paid closer attention to what was going on. I'm so sorry. By the way, your hair color turned out great and you are not a freak. You are very beautiful, Amie."

"Thank you. I like my hair very much this way."

"Come on, lets go shopping for clothes and then we'll have lunch."

We shopped to loud music with fast-paced beats. Amie really looked cute in all the latest trendy clothes. My favorite was a pair of boots that went up to her knees, a short skirt that didn't serve any purpose at all because a tunic top ended at it's hem. It showed off her well-toned, perfect legs and thighs. She topped it off with a black hat that had a military look to it. We bought several outfits, and also chose some more casual, comfortable pants and tees. We were now 'hip.'

We followed the wonderful aromas coming from a nearby sidewalk café and seated ourselves with our shopping bags placed in two other adjacent chairs. Amie translated the menu to me and I ordered a sandwich and salad.

Our waiter asked Amie in Dutch if she would like anything. She quickly replied in his language, "I do not require food." He laughed and must have thought she was being funny.

Amie looked confused, so I tried to abate awkwardness. I grinned at him, and said, "She's not hungry. Maybe just bring her a glass of water?"

After lunch, we headed for the Nordic tunnel. I had a feeling that someone was stalking us, but saw no one each time I turned around. "Amie", I said, "I think someone is following us. Can you discreetly observe them?"

She nodded and disappeared through a door to our right. Two men were suddenly walking in pace with me, one at each of my sides. I tried to turn and run back to Amie, but as I turned, they grabbed my arms, spun me back around and lifted me up off the pavement. I was carried to the curb and slammed up against a parked car. I screamed, but a large hand covered my mouth. I was pushed and pinned up against the car, unable to move.

# 14. ALIEN-SQUAMATA STEW

ONE OF THE MEN THRUST A NEEDLE into my neck. They caught me as I slumped to the pavement and they threw me into the backseat. I heard the driver shout out in pain. With my vision getting more and more blurry, I saw the driver disentegrate. Everything was spinning. The man to my right tried to scramble out of the car. I saw Amie crush his head between her hands. I felt a gun dig into my temple, but then it was gone and there was the sound of bone cracking. I passed out.

When I came to, I was in a police station, alone. I could only recall the beginning of the attempted abduction. A man in a suit proceded to question me, choosing his words very cautiously. His English was good, but he had a distinct accent. I told him I didn't know anything because I had been drugged. After an hour of this same conversation, his voice had raised sharply, and he sometimes broke into his native tongue. "You had to see something," he shouted. "You were found alone in the back seat of a car with the motor running. A man was found lying on the pavement near the backseat with his skull crushed, and another man was in the street with his neck broken. Another girl was witnessed to be at the scene, but now the observer claims he doesn't remember seeing anything, nor does he remember making the phone call to report the incident." I almost jumped out of my seat when he slammed his fist down on the table and yelled, "You must have seen something!" He had become unbearably annoying. I was about to contact Ure for help, when it all came to a halt and I was escorted out of the interrogation room. There stood Amie and Ure. They looked like a typical couple from the Amsterdam area. I found myself thinking that as tall as he was, Ure could still pass for a Dutchman.

Everyone at the station ignored me as I followed him out of the building. Once outside, I asked Amie if she was all right. She responded, "Yes, of course." I had forgotten how lethal she was.

It was at that moment I became very uneasy over the full realization of my personal situation. "Ure," I sighed, "I think I need an attitude adjustment. I'm not feeling very positive over this whole Armageddon thing. I'm scared."

"Understandably so. We knew conflict was a possible and monitored your entire day with high expectations. It was handled perfectly. Your association with the homeless person was handled wit the highest ethics as a true Enlil. You did not transform at the first sign of trouble and remained calm. Amie contacted us immediately after leaving the scene. She was aware of the observer who notified the police and rather than harm him, she let us resolve the issue. Her actions were chosen well. I arrived to ensure that today's situation was erased from the memory of the observer and the police. You need to understand that once you are fully transformed there will be no need for fear. Nothing can harm you then. Let's forget the day. How about a beer?"

Loud music and laughter drifted out from a pub on the corner. It was dark inside. We made our way to three stools that faced the windows. Ure went to the bar and ordered two tall mugs of dark ale. I heard him joke around with the bartender before bringing them to us.

At first I was nervous about blending in, but felt more relaxed after seeing some of the crowd that was coming in off the street. Anything was possible today, I thought. It was amazing how a supernatural being in a human form and ,even an android, were capable of blending into today's society without notice. Her speech pattern was a bit odd and she never ate or drank, but still, I didn't see anyone staring at her.

I sat there quietly drinking from my mug, letting it slowly smooth away all the sharp edges of the day. I now abandoned my thoughts and let my eyes wander out the window. It felt good to be a part of the human race again. The more I drank, the more I convinced myself of this. Someone tapped me on my shoulder. Amie sprang from her stool into the alert position I knew all too well.

"Hallo, spreekt heb je Nederlands?" He was wearing a green t-shirt that had "Sustain Earth" printed on it, faded jeans and an Old Navy baseball hat with its typically frayed bill. It was the fact that he resembled Brad Pitt that rendered me speechless.

It took me a couple seconds to realize he was asking me if i could speak Dutch. I mustered up an answer somehow and said, "Ik spreek niet zo goed." He spoke to me in English for a while and was very charming and fun. "It's okay, Amie," I said, still startstruck.

We began to dance. He was very entertaining, making me laugh frequently. As he spun me around, I thought I saw something way back in a dark corner of the room. He spun me again. This time I saw it clearly. I then became aware of more than one. The more we danced, the more I began to spot them. There were ten or twelve scattered around the room, lurking back in the shadows using their reptilian ability to blend into the color of the walls. Now feeling quite sober, I saw through my dance partner's hologram. I was completely surrounded. Where was Ure? It had all happened so quickly.

A bright ball of light began bouncing from wall to wall, gaining speed with each bounce. It had to be Ure. I heard, "Transform immediately." I thought about Amie, but reminded myself that she was programmed to deal with any situation. I transformed.

People shrieked as my glowing body towered over them. When I spread my wings, they screamed even louder, and scrambled out of the pub. My dance partner was now a scaled Reptilian with a long forked tongue. He hissed at me. Such a shame I had to tell him goodbye. Such a nice personality. No more drinking on the job for me.

"Dag," I said, as I thrust my finger towards him sending him airborne. He crashed into the wall. This smashed his skull, leaving a slimy, bloody trail where he slid to the floor. I remembered the small wizard-looking Nebadon's words, "Just do it!" That gift certainly worked well.

The others closed in. Ure had built up so much power that laser rays were shooting from the ball of light he had become. He was moving so fast from wall to wall that his rays were emitting with some methodical purpose, crossing the entire room while severing alien heads. Three intruders lunged at me. With an unworldly speed, I moved to the ceiling watching them fall to the floor. I then used the rays from my eyes, my second gift, to paralyze them, and watched them turn into grey clay and crumble apart. Effective! All I had to do was stare at them with the intent to exterminate.

Amie was busy slinging her black hole weaponry. Reptilian aliens were screaming everywhere as their organs, intestines, and vertebrae disappeared. Blood spewed in all directions. Guts were spilling out, covering the floor and walls with their orange and green stickiness. The last one pounced on me in an attempt to tear my neck apart with his teeth. I sent him flying across the room and then closed in on him, pointing to the middle of his scaly body. A beam of light from my finger-tip shot straight at him. My third gift became an apparent reality. I moved my finger up and down using its beam to surgically split him in two with razor sharp precision. I watched his intestines spill out revealing his three-chambered heart, liver, and gall bladder before he slid slowly down in his own blood. I certainly had been equipped like a warrior.

The entire pub was now coated in a stew-like consistency thickened with reptilian body parts. I titled our masterpiece an 'alien-squamata stew.' I sympathized with the owner of the establishment and wondered if he could file an insurance claim on this type of damage.

It was now quiet, thank goodness. The bartender hid behind

the bar and everyone esle had fled. I heard sirens approaching. Ure, Amie and I snuck out the back door. I flicked something off Amie's shoulder that resembled a blue spaghetti noodle. It wiggled aimlessly on the ground unable to return to its source. We transformed back before we exited an alley and turned right on to another street. Ure looked at me and said, "See what I mean? How do you like your special abilities?"

"I have much respect for my supernatural ancestors now," I responded.

Back at the tunnel, a new tempo prevailed inside as Nordics flew back and forth, indicating a situation had reached emergency level. I wondered what precipitated this.

"Did our bar room brawl cause this?" I asked Ure.

"No," he said. "There have been several incidents all over the world revealing the Enlil movement. On one monitor just yesterday, a Nordic witnessed a standoff in New York between five reptilians and an oriental woman. They drug her by her long hair into the back room of a gift shop. They tried to overtake her before she transformed, but failed. All the major news channels are referring to it as the worst gang massacre in history. They're describing the bodies as unidentifiable to prevent mass hysteria."

That had to have been Ting, I thought.

"So this is it? The Battle of Armageddon has begun?" I asked him.

"Not quite yet," he said. The process began in May of 1948 when Israel became a nation. Major earthquakes, tsunamis and strange weather phenomena have increased dramatically over the last ten years. This increased famine has increased as a result of migration into safer territories putting a strain on water and food supplies. Lawlessness has peaked, along with growing dissatisfaction of world leaders to solve global problems. It is clear that this generation will witness the end of the world as they know it now. We predict the Enkis will master transmitton telepathic thoughts to promote a war that could annihilate two-thirds of the human race, at the time the United States is in a state of weakened financial and political power. As you know, there are already corrupt key political figures in all the major governments of the world who will try to accelerate the alien mission. This will be implemented when China declares war on the Middle East in a matter of days now. Cosmic disturbances and signs in the heavens will signal the revelation of the antichrist to the people."

"There has been a steady rise in solar storms that result in aurora borealis to occur almost nightly now. Asteroids with precarious courses orbit regularly close to earth we monitor them constantly for possible contact with 'the keyhole,' an area of gravitational force to earth. We have isolated Appollyon, as we call him, the false Messiah, and have been observing him for some time. He has moved up from a lowly governmental roles and is presently in the race to govern three nations and become the most influential leader in all history. He is indeed charismatic and can easily fool mankind. Some refer to him as 'the Star'. This is the most powerful hybrid the Enkis have ever produced. He will resurrect the dead and promise peace to those left behind."

"So, the rapture is real, Ure?"

"Yes, of course. Your bible states in John 14:2: *'In my father's house are many mansions.'* Ours is a compulsive universe with many inhabited worlds like and unlike this Earth. Nature likes to repeat itself. The seven superuniverses co-exist with these in another dimension. Many people will be instantly transported from this planet. Mark my words, justice will then prevail and you will become part of a mighty army never before seen by man. Armageddon will be spiritual war.

It is said that when this war begins, the archangels themselves will join our forces to ensure the continuation of the human race on Earth as God intended, and once and for all end the satanic culture of combining celestial and terrestrial offspring. Do not be afraid. Your gifts when transformed are greater than those of the Enki, the fallen angels. Remember, you are a descendant of the angels who did not follow Satan, and even though your ancestors mated with the daughters of man, your spirit is supernaturally pure and therefore your special gifts are greater. We will not be defeated.

"Now I must go. There is much to do," he said. "One last thing, be prepared. There are many disembodied demons looking for hosts to posses in this one final satanic war. You will be able to see them while transformed, and you must assist the many lost and confused people wandering earth with no spiritual protection. Without our help they will be overtaken and ultimately suffer the same horrific deaths as the aliens. Things will happen quickly and life will appear to be normal on earth when it all begins to unfold."

He turned and I watched him dart to an upper level screen as a ball of light.

I had much to think about and returned to my room for a rest and a moment of reflection. "Amie, what are you doing?" I asked softly without wanting to startle her.

"I am preparing for what is already obvious," she replied.

She was holding two shining silver black hole weapons, one in each hand, as if trying them out. She turned to me and said, "It is written that the Antichrist will receive a mortal head wound and his right arm will wither. I will take out his eyes with my weapons while you send your rays to his limbs."

"Whoa, lets not get ahead of ourselves here," I said. "I doubt very seriously we will get that close to him at all."

"I think you should prepare yourself for it," she said. "A Nebadon related this to me after my assembly, before I was transported to Zio."

"Well, this is the first time I've heard anything about it," I said. "Does anyone else know of this?"

"By deductive reasoning, no, but there maybe one or two others that could be aware."


I tried to sleep that night, but he was difficult. For some reason my thoughts drifted back to my friend Hank in New Mexico. It was something he had said, but I couldn't quite remember it. I finally fell into a deep sleep after an exhausting day.

JOANNE JOHNSON

# 15. ARMAGEDDON

THE NEXT DAY proved to be one of the most dramatic and historically important days in Earth's history. Appollyon won his desired position governing over three nations, making him a key world figure and giving him the power to guide mankind into total destruction.

China has been threatening the Middle East daily a two-year dispute that directly affected them. The nations under Appollyon supported anything his wishes and the biggest disease of the modern age-deranged thinking, was alive and well, and at an all time high. Alien spacecraft began swarming over major cities of the world causing mass hysteria. People were fleeing to less populated areas to hide.

Appollyon, the Star, promised eternal peace and salvation to all would follow him. He even raised a few from the dead as a promotional gimmick. He was believed by many to be the returning Messiah the world had been waiting for. This was the beginning of the end. As predicted, the wheels were now turning swiftly in this pageant of the end of times, in which I was about to be center stage. I was nervous to the point of shaking as the full realization of my responsibilities came in to focus.

News outlets around the globe began to speak of widespread electrical and satellite disruption. This was Appollyon's cue. Miraculously, he appeared in a vision in the sky. The Nordics told me this was a hologram being sent from one of the major alien tunnels located near Dulce, New Mexico.

The next event happened in the twinkling of an eye. Massive spaceships from Nebadon appeared in the skies. They were so large, they blocked out the sun. I watched on a screen as they drew thousands, now millions of people up into their safe havens and flew away. The other screens and all the same. This was happening worldwide. A female Nordic named Rama explained to me that this was 'the rapture.' She told me that they would be taken to Zio and Nebadon for temporary food and shelter. They would be returned when the time was right. The small alien ships were shooting at the huge monstrous Nebadon crafts with absolutely no effects. They couldn't penetrate the ships and were being ignored on about the same scale as flies. What a sight.

My mood was elevating as I watched this wonderful spectacle. I knew that the Nebadon were allies. They followed through whenever they were needed. I had grown sentimentally attached to them, and this group of Nordics, just as I had the Ziots. I was thankful for their comraderie and, of course, for my best friend, Amie. My thoughts turned to my fellow Enlils all over the world. I wondered what we would do when it was all over. Would we migrate to a well chosen earthly location where we could live in peace? Or would we scatter, living as we chose separately, in whatever environment our planet changed to after all was said and done? Time was on our side, lots and lots of time. It didn't really matter now.

I began to focus again on the screens, which were still up and running by some special unknown force. There was mass hysteria everywhere, death tolls rising. People were scrambling, blocking all the major highways, shooting each other over a tank of gasoline, looting, and even committing suicide. It saddened me to see this unnecessary, self-imposed doom. Tears ran down my cheek as I thought of the children, so innocently caught up in it. My sadness turned quickly to anger. I was ready!

Ure signaled for Amie and I to follow him. The Nordics were leaving their posts and assembling together to depart the tunnel. We were directed to stand within a large circle marked on the floor of the tunnel just outside the main facility. It was the same location of our disengagement from the small flying vessel that had transported us through the long tunnel when we had first arrived. The floor began to rise slowly until we were above-ground. We were lowered to a desert-like terrain slow until we touched the ground. I was told we were in Dulce, New Mexico. I welcomed the soil beneath my feet in my favorite state and longed for my old adobe house. We were joined by several other groups of Nordics traveling in the same fashion. I ran up to Ting and we hugged.

"Was it you on the news in New York?" I asked her.

"Yes," she sighed. "Have you used your powers yet?"

I nodded. "We got in a fight with about twelve aliens not

long ago."

"I'm so glad you're alright, Ting," I said.

Several lazer rays barely missed us and interrupted our conversation. I heard, "transform now."

The Nordics were becoming balls of light. Me and mankind transformed and I lowered myself for Amie to mount on my back. We soared into the sky behind the Nordics.

A small, disc shaped spacecraft came up behind us. I turned, and thrust it into another spacecraft, which sent them both spiraling down in flames. I accelerated and soared higher. We caught up with another craft that was flying high and I jumped on top of it. As we were riding the enemy, we quickly set about eliminating the others. I was able to split most of them in two with my rays. A smoky trail gave way to a dramatized landing by one behind some tall rock formations. I decided to split the one I was still riding. With one foot on each half of it, I kept it together a while longer and spread my wings.

What a sight we were. Looking down, I saw that the pilot was still alive in his half of the craft. He began shooting at us. I used my fist and thrust his half of the craft away, letting the other half fall to the ground. We were airborne again and continued to follow the smoke to a spot where we could land on top of some rocks. I lowered myself, allowing Amie to dismount.

"This ones all yours, Amie," I said. Observing the stranded spacecraft, I saw the side open slowly. The Reptilian alien who emerged looked confused, but angry. His metallic jumpsuit seemed to be some sort of protective armor. 'A feeble attempt,' I chuckled to myself. He tried to shoot Amie with his ray gun, but she dodged every shot, jumping from the rocks, repeating cart wheels in the air, leaping toward him at blinding speed.

She landed on his shoulders, and forced him to the ground. He grabbed her leg. I moved in to help her, but she used her other leg and kicked him. He tried to grab her again, but she already had her hands on the sides of his head and blood spurted out as she crushed his skull. I shook my head in awe over the incredible magnitude of her strength.

We returned to our original formation. The other Enlils and the Nordics were gathering after combat. "This mission is complete," Ure said.

"What about the Antichrist and the others in the tunnel?" I asked.

"There are not enough left in the tunnel to waste our time on going back and as for the antichrist, I believe he is being saved for a special assignment by the archangel Michael. Just as he once chased the fallen angels away from Earth long ago, Michael also wants the final destruction of their hybrid for himself. He will then go after Satan ,banashing him into captivity on a miserable planet far away where he will suffer for eternity. When you see the brightest light in the sky you ever imagined possible, you will know the archangels have descended to assist us. Their power is ours magnified a million times."

"We have been directed to go back to Amsterdam and protect the people now. They are under attack. When we are finished there, we will assist other Nordics and Enlils wherever we are needed. There has been worldwide military attack on the aliens and our allies are doing fairly well on their own, but need our support. We know where all the opposition's tunnels are located and must concentrate our forces on them after we secure Amsterdam."

"Who gives your instructions, Ure?" I asked.

"I cannot disclose his identity to you at this time. He is our Creator's personal messenger. We refer to him as 'the Mighty One. Perhaps you will meet him someday."

# 16. MEET SATAN

WE ALL RETURNED TO THE CIRCLE that had transported us to New Mexico from Amsterdam. In the middle of the desert. I had barely visible lights traveling along the perimeter to indicate its location. In an instant, we were back in the tunnel in Amsterdam.

The screens displayed cities still suffering even more than when we had left. Buildings and cars were burning. People were out of food; and all municipal organizations were shut down, leaving humans without water, power, medical assistance, or police protection. The small alien spacecraft were whizzing about, dipping down to destroy humans whenever they were spotted. It was attempted genocide. My blood boiled at the scenes and I was ready to assist in any way possible. In fact, I couldn't wait.

Once above ground, I lowered myself for Amie to mount my back and we soared into the sky above Amsterdam. I spotted a family trying to outrun a Reptilian in a street below. His was faster and he was shooting his ray gun at them. The father was carrying a child on his back. The woman stumbled, and as the father tried to help her up, the Reptilian closed in. The father protectively placed himself in front of his family. I had seen enough. With my fist, I thrust the ugly, little, evil creature into the side of a wall. I face to face with him, only a inches between us. Achiveing eye contact, I slowly split him open, following his terror filled eyes as he slid down the wall. The father held his family and looked for shelter.

"Amie, show them to a safe place to hide for now and catch up with me afterwards. Protect them." She nodded and joined them.

I watched as she guided them to an old warehouse while, she monitored the sky in all directions. They were safe with her.

Satisfied, I flew back into the sky and locateded a craft shooting its rays at a houseboat floating down the river. Reptilians on the ground were also in pursuit of the houseboat. I sent the disc-shaped craft crashing to the ground where it exploded on impact. The aliens below were, perching on the railing of a bridge, waiting to pounce on when the houseboat floated underneath them. I heard the couple's screams when they saw the reptiles. I lowered myself to the houseboat and standing on its deck spread my wings and faced the reptiles on the bridge. This surprised them and they froze, unable to anticipate my next move. One lost his balance and fell off into the water. The entire episode was fun. My concentrated look turned into a paralyzing gaze as I turned the others into clay and watched them crumble, their pieces splashing into the water also. I thrust another down under the water with my finger until he drowned.

A shaking middle-aged man and his wife dropped to their knees and began a prayerful thanks. I lifted them up and told them "I'm just like you, so please don't praise me because I have wings. I'm not even sure how I sprouted them. Let me push your boat to a hiding place. This turmoil will all be over soon."

I tucked them away between two large tankers where they were out of sight and flew away.

I caught sight several balls of light bouncing and buildings shooting rays at Reptilians on the ground. Others were in the air destroying enemy spacecraft quite effectively. The entire city was in shambles with debris in the streets, overturned cars, and numerous fires still burning. People were hiding wherever they could. Sometimes someone would make a run to change locations or to escape from aliens who had found their hiding places. Many were dead in the streets. After helping hundreds escape and destroying a good number of spacecraft, I began to wonder about Amie.

The screams had subsided, and there were no more aliens visible in the sky or on the ground at this time, so I decided to search for her. I flew over Amsterdam from end to end, but she was nowhere to be seen. I heard Ure transmit telepathically to return to the tunnel. However, I walked the streets for perhaps another two hours looking for her. Military Jets soared in the sky patrolling the city, a little late, but with good intentions. A search helicopter could be heard above occasionally flying low. Not wanting to alarm them, I would stand near the trunk of a tree with my wings tucked close to my body so as not to cause attention to myself. I was no longer part of the human race. I had turned into a killing machine and was enjoying it.

Where had my frame of reference gone? Where were all the psychological buffers to help me adjust to all these strange experiences? I began to feel depressed.

Suddenly, I saw Amie as she rounded a building on a corner about one block north of me. She was walking slowly carrying a baby in her arms. That moment would be my point of reference for the hundreds of years I remained on Urantia. To see an android rescue a baby and lovingly carry it back to the tunnel after she had killed so many aliens in battle rescued me. As quirky as this seemed, it somehow brought me relief. There was once again meaning in my life and hope for mankind, no matter how crazy things got. I flew over to her. "Amie, I was so worried!"

"I saw his parents die and scooped him up before the Reptilians could destroy him. I've had to hide and protect his. I didn't want to leave him to go fight. Isn't he beautiful?"

I was stunned at the display of emotions Amie was capable of. "Yes, he is beautiful. Lets take his home to the tunnel." I put my arm around her and the three of us went home.


A female Nordic agreed to watch the baby while we left for another mission. This time, it was in Rome, Italy. The Italians were being slaughtered and the Vatican was up in flames. Via the travel circle, we were instantly there. Amie and I flew over the famous domed cathedral. We entered through a small wing to the south and found many robed priests slain in the hallways, many of them beheaded. All the crosses had been turned upside down. There was no one to rescue within the cathedral walls. They had all been forced out into the open and were being attacked, along with the civilians in the streets.

Reptilian spacecraft shot at them wherever they could be found. As we set out again to survey the city, we could see that the Nordics had already begun aerial battle. Amie and I flew down low, over rooftops, through tiny cobblestone streets , and between homes looking for reptiles. I detected a priest guiding a crowd into a house to hide. Several aliens were after them on foot. I dropped Amie off to sling her black hole weaponry and I perched myself on a roof to use my gifts to slaughter these ugly creatures from above. The people began coming out into the streets staring in bewilderment.

It was then I realized something was shadowing me from above like a big dark cloud. When I looked up, I saw a giant, red creature with bat-like wings outstretched and a human head with glowing red eyes staring down at me. I tried to thrust it away, but nothing happened. In fact none of my gifts worked on it, and I suspected his powers to be greater than mine. I reacquainted myself with the feeling of fear. He was without a doubt concentrating on me and remained motionless. My heart pounded; I felt paralyzed. A hideous, dark and sickening feeling emanated from this creature.

Abruptly, I was blown through the air at a tremendous speed to a deserted area covered with grass. I slowly descended by some force unknown to me. I landed softly and unhurt on the ground. I noticed a windmill strategically placed on the horizon to catch the wind from the sea. I knew the sea was just over the top of the hill and I was standing below sea level. An oddity I never quite got used to here. I looked up and saw a brilliant light in the sky slowly descending. It was blinding, and I had to shield my eyes. I had never seen anything like it. The sound of thunder permeated the air as this light descended, and flashes of lightening shot out of it in all directions. It glided towards me. At the same time, something was approaching from the opposite direction. When I felt this new presence behind me, I quickly turned to face it. It was a man. He had come over the hill and was walking towards me. He wore a black suit. They were both closing in on me.

As the man approached, I was relieved as I began to recognize him. "Hank? Is that you, Hank?" He stopped before me. His body didn't seem so frail, bony and old, but actually much stronger with a younger, athletic appearance. But he was still recognizable. He raised his right hand towards the radiant light and bowed his head. Upon closer inspection of this luminous, burning object, I could make out the faint outline of a humanoid figure.

The shape began to take on a more distingable form as and I beheld a beautiful, firey being with six silver wings. There was a single eye on each wing. This unusual, but magnificent creature lingered for approximately five seconds observing me, and then disappeared in an instant. I ran up to Hank and hugged him.

"You got yourself in a pickle back there, "he said." Are you aware of what was lingering over you?" As you perched on the roof.

"No, but I was sure it was evil encarnate and wanted to destroy me."

"You bet it did. That, my dear, was the Satan himself," he explained. He's been deceiving the world with false prophets, delusions of miracles and ideology for years. He's running out of time though.

He knows you are predicted to be a part of overthrowing his hybrid child, the AntiChrist. That's why he wanted a closer look at you – to evaluate the enemy. You see, you almost didn't make it to Zio in time. You were the very last Enlil; and the one prophesized to destroy the AntiChrist. Things are proceeding as intended. Don't worry. There are many unseen forces surrounding you and protecting you."

"Me?"

"Yep. As soon as I was aware of the plan, I began tracking you, making sure you are safe until the ugly deed is finished."

"What was that in the sky just now, Hank?"

"That was a mighty Seraphim. One of the highest order of angels in existence, part of a group of angels closest to God, often called the 'burning ones,' for obvious reasons. They are described in the Book of Enoch and the Book of Revelation. Recently, an image of a Seraphim, which is thought to date from the fourteenth century, has been rediscovered in Istanbul. The face, as you saw, is the only part resembling a human, the rest of the figure being spirit. They rarely make an appearance, but there are many variations of missions requiring them. I was told he would look after you until I arrived. It was his gust of wind that whistled you to this safe place."

"Who are you, Hank? What are you?"

"Whoa, not so fast. Let's not get in front of ourselves. Everything has a time and place. It has all been predetermined and must follow its course. I will reveal all to you soon enough, but not now. I have to go. It's safe for you to return to your android.

She is desperately searching for you, and Italy has been secured. It's almost all over."

He disappeared in a flash. I flew back to the place where I had first encountered the dragon-like creature. I pinpointed Amie who was desperatly searching the skies for me, and lowered myself to the street where she stood.

"Where have you been?" she asked, exacerbated.

"I'm not sure," I responded.

# 17. A NEW ERA BEGINS

WE DEPARTED ROME to return to our home base, the Nordic tunnel in Amsterdam. The news there on the screens and in the air, was that almost all the Enki, alien descendants of the Nephilim, the fallen angels, had retreated to their underground lairs and their numbers drastically reduced. The destruction of all the tunnels and their Antichrist, was all that remained on our agenda. A festive atmosphere prevailed.

However, the clock was ticking. Would Satan resume his rule on Urantia, possibly bring new life forms to stop humans from their birth right to evolve and dominate the Earth? Could Satan still sway things once again in his favor? We already knew he was a patient entity and secretly plotted against us. Although things seemed to be going in our favor, I felt uneasy. Something hung in the air. Was something terrible about to happen?

The Nordics, from bases all over the world had broadcast their advanced power on a global scale. The humans remaining on earth grouped together in a movement to salvage what was left, tend to the injured and dying with dignity, and restore a normal sense of life. In other words, begin again. This was the human way. Even though they weren't part of the chosen millions who had escaped the planet, there was purpose to their survival and drive to continue on. I felt sure that when the others returned, the next phase of evolution would surely procure leaders derived from wise elders of only the purest heart and mind.

Most people of the various religions especially those biblically taught were familiar with the progression of prophesized events, even though they may have not been true believers. Even though aliens, Nordics, Enlils, and androids had not been exactly spelled out many years ago as to be part of the end times, it was playing out just asdescribed otherwise. Hanks words had haunted me. I quickly looked up something in a western, Christian bible on my own handy media screen.

*He will be successful until the time of wrath is completed, for what has been determined must take place.* Daniel 11:36.

How did he forsee this? There had to be more to Hank's true identity.

Witnesses, including some who had seen Enlils flying in the sky or Nordics transforming into balls of light during the battle, were excitedly exchanging their experiences. Historians were digging up information regarding the play that was unfolding before humanity. The Nordics had picked up a telecast from London and were monitoring it. I tuned in as the screen brought attention to a speech made long ago by

Ronald Reagan when he was president of the United States in which he stated, "And yet I ask you is not an alien force already among us?" There had indeed been a few presidents interested in UFO sightings and events that hinted at the presence of visitors from space or an underworld existence of alien beings. Dwight D. Eisenhower was said to have met with them in secret. People globally had been seeing spacecraft in the skies for years, including all the way back to ancient times translated as drawings in caves and on stone.

I walked away thinking about Hank. He had said he worked for several species. I had already learned of the existence of four other dimensions and many different species of beings in a very short length of time. Our universe was teaming with life imaginable and unimaginable.

The strongest military forces of the world being trust with the possession of nuclear capability were now being anonymously informed of the locations of the worldwide underground tunnels and were preparing to crush them, buring them forever. All the nations of the world had come together in this plan. Whatever differences existed before were forgotten in pursuit to save the planet. Our world was finally, for the first time in history, at peace with eachother and uniting as one. Defense craft loaded with nuclear weapons were departing from land and sea for the tunnels. The small star-shaped aircraft were capable of movement in any direction, invisible to the naked eye, and untraceable by any equipment. They were silent and capable of extended, motionless suspension in the air at any height. They could stalk close to the ground or soar into outer space. These quickly eradicating all the tunnels, once their locations had been fully disclosed.

What we didn't know was the exact current location of their

most evil hybrid, Allelyon, the Antichrist. And what about Satan? How and when was he being banished and by whom? Who was this entity that they were being saved for?

"Come on, Amie. I have a feeling about where we can find Allelyon. We're flying to Israel."

We flew southeast from Amsterdam late that evening, wand arrived by nightfall. The white desert sand glistened in the moonlight, which gave a moist appearance. It was a clear night. I asked Amie to notify me when we had traveled approximately sixty-five miles north of Jerusalem. Once there, we rested under a palm tree in a valley under a black, star-studded sky. A tinkling bell woke me. I saw a shepherd crossing the border with his sheep. He stopped a few yards from us and nodded. We sprang up and Amie evaluated him. "He is a mirage and not really there, she said. Something is not right about those sheep. They are connected somehow and not real mammals."

"Wait until it transforms," I said. "Be very careful. He may have back up."

The ensuing events were both supernatural and strange. His sheep became a giant serpents. They flew at Amie and pinned her to the ground. A flock of ten giant black bats with shrill, high-pitched screams descended upon me and tried to scratch and peck me. I recalled them from my first, night on Zio and remembered not to make eye contact with them. One by one, I thrust them away with my fist forcing their blood-sucking, mind-draining black bodies back up into the sky. As they tumbled back down, I splashed each one in half by aiming my finger at them. With my head cocked to one side, I watched as their pieces fall to the ground. I spun around to face the shepherd who transformed into a large about eight feet tall beast with the head of a man, standing on all fours. His face was hard and rough with warts and other abnormalities that secreted puss all over the surface of his skin. His red eyes glowed as he stared at me.

Had I taken on too much alone? Let's do it! I thought.

He reared up on his hind legs and then stomped the sand with one hoof like a bull. His body was covered with shaggy, tangled brown and black fur. Suddenly, seated on a scarlet blanket on the back of the beast, a woman appeared with a flashy, cheap appearance like that of a whore. She threw her head back, laughed coarsely and spit on me. She fondled with her greasy locks of hair that fell over her shoulders. She exuded a sickening scent of cheap perfume. I gave no reaction and tried to conceal my confused state.

I struggled with the question, "Which one should I fear, the woman or the beast?"

Then the woman's face began to slowly morph increasing speed to many fast changing faces. I saw the faces semblance of prophets, religious leaders, and political leaders throughout history who had tried to confuse the world with false beliefs.

Finally, the brightly painted face of the woman stared back at me, concentrating all her attention on me. Her eyes were black and she wore red lipstick smeared sloppily on her lips. Dark red rouge adorned her cheeks. She stuck her tongue out and wagged it at me. It extended about three feet and had an eye on the tip of it. She then laughed loudly and belched, smiling and obviously delighted in her own disgusting nature. I refused to react, giving her no power. The thought came to me to slowly turn away as if to forget she was there. When I did this, she disappeared.

I had guessed at, or perhaps been inspired by the right decision. Only the beast was left. It was as I thought. Allelyon had numerous visages before he showed his true nature.

The beast roared and gnashed his sharp teeth. Thick saliva dripped out of his mouth and his hot, fowl breath burned my skin. Quickly I split the snakes in half enabling Amie's escape.

He then thundered towards me and head butted me to the ground. Amie slung her black hole weapon at the beast's eye. I frantically wiped his black blood away as it dripped from his wound on my face. I took advantage of his miserable state as he bellowed over his eye wound. I looked to my right. I saw his front left leg and quickly severed it. He fell on top of me, and I felt as if I were being crushed. I was suffocating. With great difficulty, I opened my eyes. They stung from his thick hair and blood, and I could not see. I stared straight into his body anyway, using one of my gifts, I successfully turned him into clay. He slowly became lighter as pieces of him crumbled apart and fell away. I finally stood up, feeling great relief just to be breathing again. I watched the remaining pieces of him turn into tiny particles and disappear forever into the sand.

As he disappeared, an entire army filled the sky of the same annoying bat-like creatures from before, mourning his death with screeching high-pitched sounds. They also wanted revenge. I heard laser shots and saw several android military aircraft arrive from the west successfully targeting and destroying the creatures. As the bats were being picked off, odd bizarre looking deformed creatures began to crawl up out of the sand. They chased us and grabbed our legs as we ran. I lowered myself and Amie mounted so that we could escape into the sky. I soared above the bats and the aircraft. We had had enough. All was a magical, evil representation, a mirage of Satan's supernatural powers. We were done here. All had been a magical, evil representation, a mirage of Satan;s supernatural powers. We were done here.

Amie and I had completed a milestone in the history of Urantia. I had trouble accepting what had just happened and all that it meant. "Amie, did we really do all that by ourselves? Did we just kill the anti Christ?"

"Yes, we have completed our mission. Soon the planet and its inhabitants will evolve as intended by *The One True Source of Life*."

Back on the ground, and several miles away from the last big event, we walked in silence. I put my arm around Amie and ambled for about a mile in the moonlight, digesting our great accomplishment and savoring once again the quiet and peacefulness of the desert.

Suddenly it appeared as if all the stars were falling to earth. Asteroids from every direction hit the planet, some close to where we stood. Fire consumed everything around us and the planet felt as if was spinning faster and faster. Amie and I were pinned to the ground with gravity so intense we couldn't move.

There was something else coming; I could barely see it through the flames. It was thick, somewhat transparent; like water, but not liquid. It swept right through us and continued on its own appointed agenda. As it moved, it put out the fires and I could see the stars once again in the sky. We stood up and began walking. It was as if we had stepped into another world. Vivid, wondrous colors, some I had never seen before were everywhere. Plants, trees, creeks, and mountains filled with life. The sky was a glorious golden color. Animals grazing and colorful birds filled the landscape. This was more than I could have ever had imagined.

Giant spacecraft appeared overhead. The Nebadons were gently lowering humans to the ground. I looked at Amie and said, "Do you see them changing?"

"Yes," she responded. "They are transforming into a different species. They no longer need legs to move, and thought is their life support."

A man floated up to us and said without using words, "Isn't this wonderful?"

I didn't know how to respond. He acknowledged me as an Enlil, a Watcher, and wasn't shocked by my appearance. Instead he sent forth a feeling of acceptance and thankfulness. He knew I was a guardian of Urantia.

The people drifted off and the Nebadon ship departed without a sound.

We continued to walk with no plan. It felt strange not having a feeling of urgency. We had walked about three more miles when a bright fire appeared in the sky in the distance. As it got closer, I had to cover my eyes. It was blinding. As the fire subsided, I saw the faint outline of a tall, muscular man inside a white gaseous, cloud-like substance. He was at least nine feet tall with a brilliant, silver, steel-like body that demanded reverence and fear at the same time. He was unworldly, but magnificent. As the cloud disappeared, I saw he held a sword which he lowered as he glided towards us. The sword sparkled as if made from diamonds and precious jewels. I stepped back, unsure of his identity and purpose.

He stopped in front of us. When he spoke, his words made me tremble. He a powerful entity, a warrior of some sort I guessed.

"I am Mikha'el," he said. "I am the archangel responsible for this planet and its safety. However, my duty here is complete now that I have banished Satan. He is finished here and will never return. I will be retireing to my home and eternal dwelling place, the superuniverse nearest to the Hovana. You and the other Enlils the Watchers will continue to safeguard Urantia. Enjoy your new life. There are many wondrous miracles and experiences ahead for you. Your android will remain your lifetime companion. There is a child who needs you now. He has evolved as all the others have and will bring forth many other beings to complete your new family. I enjoyed our friendship and will never forget you."

"What? I don't understand," I said, but he had already disappeared.

"Hank? Are you Hank?"

www.ingramcontent.com/pod-product-compliance
Lightning Source LLC
Chambersburg PA
CBHW051832170626
46807CB00003B/1146